"He went rig said, droppi **couch next t proper dist** course.

"I sat with him about five minutes—thought he might ask some questions about why he was going to keep on living with me for a little while, or maybe talk about the Christmas tree. But he just turned over on his side and went to sleep. It was a big day for him. I think we actually wore him out."

"He's had a turbulent life so far. As far as the Christmas tree goes, I have an idea he's learned not to count on anything. If you don't count on it, you don't end up being disappointed." Fallon raised her mug of hot chocolate to her lips, but paused before she took a sip. "It's not a mistake, is it? Giving him this big Christmas?"

He laughed. "Giving a child a big Christmas? I think it's the best thing we can do for him. Tyler needs something to look forward to in his life. I don't think he's ever really had that."

"You, too," she added. "You need something to look forward to."

"And what about you? What do you need, Fallon?"

Dear Reader

Welcome to the third book in my *Mountain Village Hospital* series. I've really enjoyed writing this story because I love old steam locomotives, and I've featured one in my story. It's called *The Christmas Train*. I was fortunate enough to ride this train a couple of years ago. The steam engine was dated 1923, as were the cars. It was an amazing ride. A little bumpy. Quite loud. But so much fun because this was the original train that skirted the rim of the mountains in this area and, except for a bit of maintenance, the train was unchanged since 1923. It even had an old-fashioned black pot-bellied stove in the cars for heat.

So my husband and I, along with my husband's parents, took this little train trip, and the whole time I kept thinking how I wanted to use this beautiful little train in one of my books. Why? Because my grandmother loved riding trains, and she was riding the rails back in 1923. For just a while I got to experience something my grandmother loved, something she'd done, and it was amazing stepping back in time. For me, it was a wonderful, unexpected Christmas gift.

At this time of the year there are so many fun, exciting things to do. Be good to yourself and, if you're able, reconnect to something you've loved from your past. That would be my fondest wish for you this holiday season.

Wishing you health and happiness

Dianne Drake

PS: I'd love to hear about your experiences of reconnecting to something beloved from your past. Feel free to e-mail me at Dianne@DianneDrake.com

CHRISTMAS MIRACLE: A FAMILY

BY
DIANNE DRAKE

MILLS & BOON

All the characters in this book have no existence outside the imagination of the author, and have no relation whatsoever to anyone bearing the same name or names. They are not even distantly inspired by any individual known or unknown to the author, and all the incidents are pure invention.

First published in Great Britain 2010
Harlequin Mills & Boon Limited,
Eton House, 18-24 Paradise Road, Richmond, Surrey TW9 1SR

© Dianne Despain 2010

ISBN: 978 0 263 87929 2

Harlequin Mills & Boon policy is to use papers that are natural, renewable and recyclable products and made from wood grown in sustainable forests. The logging and manufacturing process conform to the legal environmental regulations of the country of origin.

Printed and bound in Spain
by Litografia Rosés, S.A., Barcelona

Now that her children have left home, **Dianne Drake** is finally finding the time to do some of the things she adores—gardening, cooking, reading, shopping for antiques. Her absolute passion in life, however, is adopting abandoned and abused animals. Right now Dianne and her husband Joel have a little menagerie of three dogs and two cats, but that's always subject to change. A former symphony orchestra member, Dianne now attends the symphony as a spectator several times a month and, when time permits, takes in an occasional football, basketball or hockey game.

Recent titles by the same author:

CHAPTER ONE

FALLON O'GARA glanced at her watch, and the panic in her rose a little more than she'd expected. It was ten after one now, and she was late to meet her good friends and colleagues Gabby Ranard and Dinah Ramsey for lunch. Yet she couldn't bring herself to open the car door because she was about to take a big step, and it scared her. She'd fretted, paced, worried all night, and now it was time. Time to make a decision about Gabby's job offer, and finally think about returning to work for the first time since the plane crash. But she couldn't lay her hand on the doorhandle, let alone open the door and get out.

A loud tapping on the passenger's side window startled Fallon out of her dilemma. It was Gabby, standing there with Dinah. "I'm coming," Fallon called without opening her window, without making the slightest motion toward getting out.

"We've got the back table reserved," Gabby yelled. "And you know Catie. She can't wait to see you. She's standing at the front door right now, ready to cry." To prove her point, Gabby stepped back and pointed to the café owner standing with hankie in hand, on the verge of blubbering.

Fallon loved these people! They were the best. But being here at Catie's Overlook, her favorite restaurant in the world, was suddenly feeling like a mistake. She wanted to go in, wanted to accept that job offer Gabby had made to set up the practical details of White Elk's new women's hospital—buy the beds, hire the staff, hire the contractors to make the renovations. It was a kind, generous offer, since she'd told Gabby that she wasn't ready to go back to nursing at the main White Elk Hospital. But she was afraid to accept Gabby's offer. Afraid not to. Not sure what to do. Consequently, her hands were shaking, her breath was clutching in her lungs. But surviving an airplane crash… there were always the reminders, and for her one of them was the panic attacks.

Gabby took another step toward the front of the car, and simply smiled at Fallon. "Well, darn," Fallon muttered to herself. "Having lunch with my best friends should be an easy thing to do. I'll simply get out, go in, say…." Well, she wasn't sure what she'd say to Gabby, and Gabby did want an answer. "I'll eat, chat, go home." And forty-five minutes later, well into a heaped piece of chocolate cake, she still wasn't sure what she was going to say to Gabby.

"Well, should I order a celebratory flute of ginger ale?" Gabby finally asked. Gabby wasn't drinking alcohol as she had a baby on the way. "Assuming your answer to my offer is yes? And if it's not, could you explain that to little Mary here, because her mommy needs rest at this stage of the pregnancy and if you don't take this job, little Mary's mommy is going to be worn out by the time little Mary's born."

"Good guilt trip," Dinah commented, laughing.

Gabby patted her belly, smiling. "Just using what I have to, to get my way." She looked over at Fallon. "Seriously, I really do need you. Not because of my pregnancy but because of your skills. I trust you to do this job and do it well."

Fallon sighed. Her back was to the wall now; she had to be fair to Gabby. Yes, or no? She wanted a voice from the heavens to cry out the answer, but when none came, she braced herself, trying to force aside the awkward tension attempting to burrow its way out. It was a job made to order. One where she could build up some confidence, still be close to medicine, and work her life out from that point forward. Also, this was something she could do on her own terms. If ever there was an opportunity to step back into her life, the way it used to be, the way she wanted it to be again, this was it. And it was true what they said about the very first step being the hardest.

Looking into the faces of her friends, and over at Catie, the owner of the restaurant, she realized just how *not* alone she was in this. And it was time. She'd isolated herself for too long now. Months in rehab then hiding out in her cabin. She'd been through so much. But now was the right time to begin again. Suddenly, it all made sense. Surviving came in steps. It didn't happen the way most people believed, in one great event or whoosh. It trickled in, a little here, a little there. This was one of those trickles. Although a big one. But when she realized that it was what she had to do and, more than that, wanted to do, a sense of calm fell over Fallon, the first real calm she'd felt in months. So, she reached across the table and squeezed Gabby's hand. "Order the ginger ale. I'm ready to celebrate. And promise me you'll tell little Mary that I'll be making sure her mommy will get all the rest she needs for the rest of her pregnancy."

"Really? You're going to take the job?"

Fallon nodded, wondering if what she was feeling now was the calm before the storm. "I'll try, Gabby. That's the best I can give you right now. But I'm going to take it a day at a time, because that's about the only way I can handle my life. So, if that's agreeable to you and little Mary, I'll start work as soon as you want me to."

Gabby winked at Dinah. "Told you so."

"You were betting on me?" Fallon asked.

"Just the chocolate cake," Gabby said, "and it's Dinah's treat. She was pretty sure you'd eventually say yes, but she thought it would take more persuasion."

Fallon laughed. "In that case, I'm going to order another piece to take home with me."

It felt good being there with friends, being involved in something again. She glanced out the window to the Three Sisters. She'd avoided looking at them since she'd been home, didn't want to be reminded that her plane had crashed on the Middle Sister. Popular Indian lore said these three mountain peaks loomed over the valley, protecting everybody in their shadow. People here truly believed that. To be honest, she'd believed it too, until the accident. Now, to her, the Three Sisters were simply mountains. Yet in the brief glance she allowed herself she was surprised she wasn't panicking. So maybe going back to work *was* a good thing. Maybe the calm she was feeling was real. She wanted it to be.

"Bet or no bet, I'm glad you're doing this," Dinah said, putting her fork down halfway though her cake. "Eric and Neil are going to be thrilled." Eric Ramsey was Dinah's husband and Neil Ranard was married to Gabby; both men were doctors and co-owners of the White Elk Hospital.

The three friends chatted on, until suddenly they were interrupted.

"Fallon?" The familiar, deep voice cut through the talking at the table.

Fallon gasped. Felt her pulse double immediately. She hadn't seen or spoken to James in months, since just after her accident, when she'd made it clear that she couldn't be in a relationship with him any more. Because he'd just discovered he had a son, and she'd had plenty of her own issues to deal with, things she couldn't talk to James about. She'd done what she'd thought was best for both of them. But she was just taking her first steps back into normal life and she didn't feel like she could deal with James now.

"Fallon, how are you?"

Suddenly, her lungs felt so tight that she couldn't breathe and her hands were shaking so hard her muscles were practically seizing up. On top of it all, she was breaking out in a cold sweat. Head spinning. Chest aching. Nausea fast on the rise.

"Fallon?" Gabby whispered, leaning into her. "Are you OK?"

"Tell him to go away," she whispered. "Please, I don't want to see him."

Gabby looked back at Dr. James Galbraith, not sure what to make of this. "I don't know what to tell you, James. She doesn't want to see you."

"Please," Fallon begged, refusing to turn around and look at him. "Just go away, James."

"You didn't return my calls," he said, as if there were no other women sitting at the table. He stepped forward, stood directly behind Fallon and bent down. "We spoke soon after the accident, when I told you about my son. But then I called every day, for weeks, left messages on your voice mail until you canceled that number, and you never returned my calls. E-mails bounced back."

"I was a little busy," she said, turning her head away from him. "And I did leave you a message."

"*Once*. You said you were fine, that you were in a nice rehab facility, to please not bother you again. Then the next time I called I got the message that your cellphone number was no longer in use."

She scooted down in her chair, wanted to crawl under the table. "What are you doing in White Elk?" she asked.

"James is the new pediatrician at the hospital," Dinah commented. "He applied months ago, back when you were…" She stopped, glanced helplessly at Gabby.

"I'm so sorry, Fallon," Gabby said. "I wanted to tell you…but not yet. Neil and Eric hired James a while back, pending the completion of the new pediatrics wing. Now that it's completed, James is head of Pediatrics."

"And no one told me?"

"How could we?" Gabby said. "Fallon, you'd turned your back on everyone. Practically went into seclusion. And you made it clear to everyone that your relationship with James was over. But he was already hired before we knew that, and Neil and Eric weren't going to go back on their commitment to him. They wanted James from the moment they read his résumé. Knew he was perfect for the job. But with what you'd gone through…how *could* we tell you he'd moved here?"

Fallon looked up at James. "Why did you leave Salt Lake City? Why did you move here?" she asked.

"White Elk is where I wanted to be, Fallon. The way you talked about it when we were together, then what I found out about the hospital, how good it was, what a dynamic pediatric department they were setting up…"

"And me? Did I factor into that anywhere?"

Taking the cue, Gabby and Dinah slipped away from the table, not even seen by Fallon as they hurried out the door.

"Yes. At first, when I thought we were going to be together… Well, after we drifted apart, I still wanted to be here because the more I learned about White Elk, and the more I knew the reputation of the hospital, the more

I wanted to work here. You knew how bad my job was in Salt Lake…the hours, the demands. It was driving me crazy. I wasn't advancing, wasn't getting to practice the kind of medicine I wanted because I was always the backup for my medical partners. And this…it was everything I've ever wanted in my medical practice and I couldn't walk away from it just because you'd walked away from me. But I didn't mean to upset you over it because, well…I thought we could still work things out between us."

"No, we can't." She started to twist, to look at him, but caught herself in time. Oh, how she wanted to look, though. To remember, to lose herself in him. Tall, with sandy blond hair and the most gorgeous blue eyes…eyes as clear as a mountain lake. But she couldn't. Wouldn't. She'd loved this man. Had wanted to spend a life with him. Then she'd let him down in ways he could never know about, ways that were so painful to her she didn't want to be reminded of what she'd done.

James straightened up, squared his shoulders, cleared his throat to break the tension of that awkward moment. "You wouldn't talk to me, Fallon. Wouldn't let me talk to you. I know you must have gone through hell after the accident, but you just withdrew from me. All that time we'd spent together in Salt Lake City…all the plans we were making. I thought we had something that would endure. Then after the plane crash…" He paused, swallowed hard. "I know I got busy with Tyler. And I know the timing was terrible, finding out I had a son just a week after the plane crash. One day I'm not a father and the next I've got a five-year-old son whose been literally dropped on my doorstep. I'll admit I was reeling from it, not handling it as well as I should. Is that why you stayed away from me, why you didn't even let me know where you were? Is it because I had to spend so much time with Tyler when you were facing so many problems? Did I hurt you, Fallon? Because I never meant to."

"You didn't hurt me," she said. "I told you at the time that I understood how much Tyler needed you, that I was fine by myself."

But there were also things that she hadn't told James... A few weeks before the plane crash she'd discovered she was pregnant. She'd been excited, because they'd even talked about having a family, even though they hadn't dated for long. And after they'd met when she'd been transferring a patient to the hospital in Salt Lake City where James worked, their relationship had developed quickly. But, still, the pregnancy had felt very soon. So Fallon had waited for the right moment to tell him the news. But the stress level of his job had been on the rise, and he had been working so many hours, had been tired, grumpy... So she'd kept it to herself, waiting for the right moment when things had calmed down for him.

Then the plane crash as she'd been returning home to White Elk, the surgeries, the anesthesia, the doctor's discouraging prognosis of her pregnancy, and...Tyler. To add to James's stress, he'd found out he was a father to a five-year-old he'd never known about. Everything had felt so confusing, and she had been in such bad shape. In his defense, James had been too. She had seen it. Felt how he'd been so torn between wanting to be with her and needing to be with his son, a child who desperately needed a good father. So she'd kept her secret, and never told James that she'd carried his son for six months and delivered him stillborn. And now it was too late.

Through those awful months, she'd kept telling herself she couldn't add to James's burden. Kept telling herself that she was doing the right thing by him and Tyler. Because if he'd known what she was going through, he wouldn't have left her side. But Tyler had needed him, too. *Needed him more.*

"No, you didn't hurt me, James. You'd never do that. But Tyler had to be your priority. If we'd stayed together, you'd have torn yourself up trying to divide your time between Tyler and me, and it had to be about Tyler. There wasn't any other choice you could make." That was something she had come to understand more than anything else about that time. James *had* to be a father first and if she'd stayed with him, that couldn't have happened. He'd have been too divided.

"But you couldn't have told me how you were feeling, how you were afraid I'd spend too much time with you and not enough with Tyler? We couldn't have talked about it?"

She shook her head, couldn't tell him that what she would have needed from him would have been too great. She'd survived the plane crash, but in so many little pieces. James would have wanted to be the one to put those pieces back together again, and the timing…it couldn't be helped. He'd just met Tyler. And only just learned how it truly felt to love a child so desperately.

And she'd lost hers…theirs. Lost her baby before James ever knew he existed. And not telling James, not letting him be part of those few months she carried their baby, was the unpardonable sin. Not letting him be there at the delivery of their son, and hold him the way she'd been allowed to for those brief moments… It was all too late now. What was done was done. She couldn't go back and change it, and she refused to go forward and hurt James. He didn't deserve that. And she…she didn't deserve a man as good as James. "I disappeared because I had issues to resolve, and physical problems to work out."

"Without me," he said. "Even after what we'd been to each other, you wanted to do it without me?"

"Our relationship was still new, James. A few weekends. Good weekends, and that unbelievable week together, lots of long phone calls in between. Plans, expectations and excitement. But it was so much, and so fast. After the crash I had time to think about it, to realize that…"

"That you didn't love me? Because you'd said you did."

"Maybe we were confusing our emotions." She hated this, hated saying something that wasn't true because she'd known quickly into their relationship that James was the one. But she'd gone so far beyond that now, and there was no way back. "Maybe what we thought we had wasn't real."

"I don't believe that, Fallon," he snapped. "Not a word of it. But if that's the way you want to do this between us…"

"Not *us*, James. Not any more. But since you're in White Elk now, we can still be friends…"

"And you think that's enough?"

"I think it's all there is." Not all she wanted, but all she could have.

"You're wrong, Fallon. I can see it in your eyes. Something you're not saying. Something you want to say to me, but won't."

She shut her eyes. Drew in a steadying breath, and pushed herself away from the table. "You're the one who's wrong. I've said everything I want to say. And now there's nothing else."

Drawing back from her, he studied her for a moment. "That first time I saw you in Salt Lake City, when you were transferring a patient to the hospital, I knew, Fallon. Knew that if I were the marrying kind, you'd be the kind

I'd want to marry. Then you turned me into the marrying kind. I didn't change my life and my entire outlook on a whim. I changed because I knew you, even in a short time I knew you, and knew you were the one worth making those changes for. You were so amazing and open and honest, and you went after life in such a big way. And I don't believe you've changed. Maybe you believe you have, but you're not the one standing here, looking at the same woman I saw back then. I am looking at her, though, and what I'm seeing more than anything else is…confusion. Pain."

The most open, honest woman…well, not any more. But to be honest would be to wound him in so many ways and, no matter what he said, she couldn't bring herself to do that. She just couldn't. So she stood and left the restaurant without another word. Without looking back. Without letting him see the tears.

CHAPTER TWO

"OK, HE lives here now," she reasoned as she stepped out of her front door for her morning walk. "A lot of people live here that I never see, and just because he's working here it doesn't mean that I'll have to run into him." In fact, knowing he was here was good because she could go out of her way to avoid him. Catie's Overlook was out now because, apparently, he lunched there. Of course, returning to White Elk Hospital wasn't going to happen now, no matter how much Eric and Neil wanted her back, as that's where James worked. But Gabby had offered her a permanent job at Three Sisters Women's Clinic and Hospital, and in time she might be able to face nursing duty there. Someday, when she wasn't so sensitive to mothers with new babies.

The good thing was, James should rarely have reason to be there. "It could work," she concluded. Then, in time, after she'd avoided him enough, the habit would sink in. Yes, that's the way it would be. Or else she couldn't stay in White Elk. And the thought of leaving was more than she could bear. But, realistically, it was a choice she might have to make.

It was a brisk morning. Just a few weeks away from Christmas, snow was beginning to pile up higher in the mountains, and it wouldn't be long before it found its way down to the lower elevations in more than just sprinkles and showers. She loved crisp mornings like this, when her breath was visible in white puffs, when the glistening of frost on the trees looked like diamonds. Heavy sweaters, snow boots, mittens and hot chocolate…her favorite things of the season, and she was glad she was well enough to be part of it. For a time she hadn't been sure that would happen, hadn't been sure she'd ever see anything outside the gray cement block walls of the rehab hospital. Those had been bleak days, days full of so much pain and so little hope. But finally coming home, especially at this time of year…

"How far do you go now on your morning walks?"

He startled her, and Fallon immediately retreated for her front door.

"You don't have to run from me," James said. He was standing at the edge of her cottage, his hand shielding his eyes, staring up at the Older Sister. "Wasn't it you who said, just yesterday, that we could still be friends?"

"What are you doing here?" she said abruptly.

"Taking a walk, *with a friend*. You got me into the walking habit, and it's something I look forward to in the mornings now. I thought maybe we could walk together, the way we used to. Just as friends, like I said."

"I walk alone," she snapped.

He turned to face her, the clean, sharp lines of face now coming into her full view. "But I thought you were open to having a friend? And the truth is, I really need a friend because I don't really know anybody here in White Elk, except you. So I thought it would be nice if the two of us could…"

"No, it wouldn't be nice," she said, trying to avert her eyes from him, trying not to let herself get caught up in what she knew would so easily catch her. "And I don't

know why you're doing this to me, James. I made it clear
that I can't get involved with you again."

"I'm sorry, Fallon. If I have to say that a million times
before you believe me, that's what I'll do. I'm so sorry.
We both went through a difficult time but I never meant
to hurt you. And I know you say I didn't, but I must have
in some profound way."

His voice was so kind, so sincere, so agonizingly patient
it nearly melted her heart. "You didn't hurt me, James,"
she whispered, turning away. But he caught her by the arm
and turned her back to him.

"Then what is it? For God's sake tell me, so I can make
it right."

"There's nothing to make right. I...I've changed since
the accident. And now all I'm trying to do is get on with
my life. There's nothing more to say about it, James.
There's nothing left of the *us* you want us to be. I can't
be anything you want. I don't have anything left that we
wanted together."

He sighed deeply. "So maybe all I want right now is
a companion on a nice morning walk. Is that asking too
much?"

She looked up at him again. "And Tyler?"

He shrugged. "I don't know. Haven't seen him for
a couple of months. Don't even know where he is. His
mother came and took him back for the second time, and
I've been looking ever since."

Her heart broke for him, and she knew that being near
him, trying to be his friend or even a casual acquaintance
wouldn't work because she would be compelled to tell him
the truth at some point. And break his heart even more.
"I'm sorry it's not working out for you."

"So am I. He's my son. I have the right to be a part of
his life. But Shelly keeps taking that away from me."

Dear God, it hurt him, hurt her. And she didn't want to keep doing this, over and over. But their circumstances were what they were. She'd made a bad choice and nothing about it could be changed. "We can't do this, James."

"I'm not doing anything, Fallon, but asking to take a walk with you. That's all. Just a walk. This morning. No expectations attached to it. I mean, aren't you the one who told me it was so much nicer having someone to walk with? Remember that?"

She had said that, during the most wonderful time of her life, hadn't she? Back before having James so close to her was a painful reminder of so many losses. "Walking, no talking. Those are my terms. And so you'll know, I walk two miles out then two miles back. The first part is uphill, at a brisk pace. I won't slow down for you. If you can keep up with me, fine. If not, the trail is clearly marked and you won't have any difficulty finding your way back."

Rather than be dissuaded, as she'd hoped he would be, he simply chuckled.

"What's so funny?" she asked.

"You. You haven't changed a bit. That's exactly the same thing you told me the first time we walked together—except the part about walking and not talking. But if you recall, I kept up pretty well for someone who wasn't used to executing a vigorous morning constitutional the way you were."

"I slowed down for you that time," she said, spinning around and heading off down the path at the side of her cottage. Heading quite vigorously, as James would call it. "This time I won't."

"And this time you don't have to." He caught up to her in several easy strides, matching her pace perfectly. "I'm in better shape, thanks to a very good teacher who convinced me about the merits of regular exercise."

She didn't answer him.

He chuckled. "You're not going to be easy, are you? Of course, I didn't expect that you would be. But I want to make this work between us, Fallon. Want to try it again. Start slow and steady and see what happens from there."

"You can do whatever you want, James. I can't stop you. But just be clear, you'll be doing it by yourself because I'm done with us."

"Because you've met someone else? Is that it?"

She was still at the point in this break-up, so raw from it, that she believed there could never be anybody else. She'd believed that the first time he'd kissed her, the first time he'd held her hand, the first time they'd made love. And while she didn't want to, she still did believe that. Especially now that he was here, now that the memories were so vivid. "There's no one else," she told him. "Just me, and I've changed." In deep, profound ways.

That's all she said, and they spent the next four miles in total silence. Fallon didn't speak, neither did James. For which she was grateful. It was nice having him tagging along, though. Felt normal. As normal as she'd felt in all these months. Then the walk ended and he made no pretense of wanting anything more. She expected he'd ask to come inside her cottage for some reason…a glass of water, or a cup of hot tea. She even thought he might allude to seeing her same time, same place tomorrow. But he didn't. When they reached her house he gave her a very casual "Thanks for letting me walk along" then trotted away.

OK, so maybe she was a little disappointed. Largely, though, she was relieved. It's what she wanted, what she demanded now. The only way she could deal with Dr. James Galbraith, and survive.

"And then I want to go on the Christmas train. They have hot chocolate, and we can feed the reindeer. And see the dinosaurs. They have lights on them."

"The dinosaurs have lights?" James teased, popping the stethoscope from his ears.

"All colors. But we can't get close 'cause they might be real."

"What might be real? The lights, or the dinosaurs?"

The freckle-faced six-year-old giggled. "The dinosaurs, silly."

"So the lights might not be real?"

Matthew Brower, or Matty as he insisted on being called, scrunched up his nose, trying to figure out the answer to James's question. "I think they're real, too," he finally said as James helped him down off the exam table. "That's why they light up...I think."

James tousled Matty's curly white-blond hair. "Sounds like the Christmas train is going to be fun. Do they allow adults to ride on it?"

Matty shrugged. "Just moms and dads, I think. Maybe grandpas and grandmas, too."

Well, for this month, and who knew for how long, that didn't include *him*. Didn't matter. Without Tyler, and worried about Fallon the way he was, James wasn't in a very festive mood for the holidays, anyway. "You have fun, Matty," he said, "and watch out for those dinosaurs. Especially the ones with the red lights. They're the tricky ones."

Matty rolled his eyes at James, like that was a fact every sensible person on the planet already knew, then he skipped out of the exam room while James gave final instructions to Mrs. Brower. Limited activity for another few days, plenty of rest, continue taking his antibiotics, and by the beginning of the week Matty's bronchitis would be completely gone. "Call me if you have any questions," he told her on the way out the door, "and if you don't mind, I'd like you to bring him in one more time so I can listen to his chest again. As a precaution. Just stop by when it's convenient, no need to make an appointment."

No appointment. He liked that. Wasn't used to the laid-back way medicine was practiced here, but he did like it. Looked forward to a long association. Though that was still pretty much up in the air, because if he truly made Fallon's life miserable by being here, he would rethink his decision.

"I think Matty's on the mend," Dinah Ramsey commented, as she passed James in the hall.

"On the mend and excited by something called the Christmas train...it has dinosaurs."

Dinah chuckled. "That's all my daughters have been talking about for weeks. Apparently, it's a big tradition here in the valley. For two weeks, it's a Christmas train for the children then for the next few months it's an old-fashioned steam locomotive taking skiers from slope to slope."

"Quaint," James said.

"Do you ski?"

"Sometimes. When I have someone to ski with."

"Fallon might be up to it, at least on the gentle slopes. I know she spent all her time on skis before..." Dinah stopped herself. "I guess that's not the best suggestion to make, is it?"

"It's awkward. But I'll have to get used to it."

"We all understand, James. It's been tough on every-body. Fallon's like an institution in White Elk. Everybody depended on her so much I think she was probably taken for granted in the past. Getting along without her is a tough adjustment on everybody at the hospital, and it's hard to know what to do around her sometimes. You know, like treading on eggshells. And your situation with her..."

"I think she's made it perfectly clear there is no situation."

Dinah gave his arm a sympathetic squeeze. "I'm sorry. For both of you. I hope it gets easier for you in time."

Time…something he had plenty of. He was a doctor and he was…nothing else. That's all there was. Six months ago he'd pictured himself as a man who'd be married by Christmas. And now… "I hope so, too," he told Dinah before Emoline Putters, the irascible ward clerk, shooed him off to his next appointment.

"Mrs. Shelly Geary, and her son Tyler," Emoline announced, shoving the chart into his hands. "She claims the boy has a cough, but I haven't heard him."

A surge of excitement shot through James, followed by a surge of anger and the dread he'd come to know so well. So it was starting over. Except this time he wasn't giving up. He was ready to fight for Tyler. Ready for a different ending to this chapter in his life. Maybe he couldn't win Fallon back, but he sure as hell was going to win custody of his son.

"How are you doing, Tyler?" James said, putting on a happy face when he walked into the exam room. He wanted the boy to smile, to be happy to see him again. Wanted to hug the boy. But that wouldn't be the case today. Both times before, when Shelly had dropped him off, Tyler had been sullen. Nothing had changed. Still, James's heart swelled the instant he saw his son because the last time Shelly had taken him away, he wasn't sure he'd ever see Tyler again.

"James," Shelly said, without the least bit of concern in her voice.

"In the hall!" he demanded, then exited the room.

She followed. "It's not like you think—" she started.

But James interrupted her. "What's different this time? Does Donnie want to keep him and *you're* the one who doesn't want him?" Donnie, the husband who didn't want to raise a son that wasn't his. That was the reason she'd brought Tyler to him the first two times and he had no reason to believe that wasn't the reason this time.

"You've got it all wrong. Donnie tries really hard, but Tyler gets on his nerves. And Donnie's got this new job now…"

"Save it, Shelly. I don't care about your excuses, and I sure as hell don't care about your husband." Two nurses in the hall raised eyebrows, and then James led Shelly into the empty exam room across the hall and slammed the door shut. "The only one who's important here is Tyler, and I'll swear if you've…"

"Tyler doesn't even try, James. He breaks things, and throws tantrums. Donnie works hard, and when he comes home at night he wants peace and quiet. Doesn't he have a right to have peace and quiet in his own home?"

A million things crossed James's mind, things he wanted to say, things he wanted to scream. But he wouldn't because none of it mattered. At the end of the day, all he cared about was Tyler and, God willing, he was going to get permanent custody of him this time. "Look, just get out of here. I don't give a damn why you're dropping him off, don't give a damn what Tyler's doing to make your husband angry."

"It won't be long, James. Just through the holidays, maybe, then things will settle down."

Things would never settle down for Shelly and, no

matter what else happened, Tyler wasn't going back into that situation. Not after the holidays, not ever, if he had his way. "Get out, Shelly. Get out of White Elk." With that, he brushed around her and went straight back to the exam room where Tyler was sitting. And shut the door. Shelly wouldn't come back, wouldn't say goodbye to her son. He knew that from history.

So did Tyler.

"I'm sorry, Dr. Galbraith, but I just can't do it. He wore me out chasing after him, and it's only been half a day. He's too…destructive, and I simply can't have him in my house." As proof, Mrs. Prestwick held up the headless porcelain figurine Tyler had broken. That, and the lamp for which James had already compensated her. "I hate to give you such sort notice, but you can't bring Tyler back here." Emphatic words. The same words he'd heard from Mrs. Powers and Grandma Addy…the three most highly recommended care-givers in White Elk. Three days, three bridges burned, and James was at his wit's end now. He had to work, had to take care of Tyler and, at this moment those two parts of his life were clashing in a big way. "I don't suppose you could recommend anyone else, could you?" he asked the gray-haired septuagenarian.

She shook her head, backing away from her front door as hastily as she could, practically shutting the door in James's face. He looked down at Tyler, who seemed preoccupied by the snowflakes falling on the evergreen bushes. "I thought you were going to behave," he said, trying to be patient. "We talked about it the last time you stayed with me and we talked about it just this morning. Remember? Remember how you promised me that you would be good?" For Mrs. Powers it had been about a dozen raw eggs and a pound of ground coffee, all stirred into a nice little cake in the middle of her kitchen floor…a floor that had enough slope that it had facilitated the slithering of that mess to a spot underneath the refrigerator, which had required James to move the fridge and do the cleaning. For Grandma Addy it had involved the hiding of her hearing aid in the trash can just before the trash had been tossed out. Luckily, Grandma Addy had a spare, but James was going to have to take time off work to take her to Salt Lake City and get fitted for another.

"Tell me, Tyler, why did you break Mrs. Prestwick's things?" He wanted to understand him. Wanted to get to know him and find out why he did what he did, but so far Tyler had resisted pretty much every effort James had made, just like the two previous times when James had taken care of him.

Tyler shrugged, still more interested in the snow-flakes.

James huffed out the impatient sigh he'd tried holding in. Three days, and he was all out of ideas. Yet he couldn't get angry with Tyler. In spite of everything, he loved his son and didn't blame him for the bad behavior. It was a reaction to his life, to the way he'd been tossed around. Sadly, as hard as James tried to be responsive to Tyler, the boy always pulled away from him. First time, second time and this time. Nothing about that had changed. Nothing about the fact that he'd missed the first years of Tyler's life would change and he wondered if he'd known about Tyler all that time, if he'd had a hand in raising him, in being his dad, whether Tyler would be so destructive now. Things to wonder about, but things he'd never know since Shelly hadn't told him about Tyler until her husband had forced her into it. "Well, for now you're going to have to come back to work with me." And do what? James didn't have a clue. Not a single, solitary clue. "Look, Tyler, I don't know what it is you've got against these women, but we need to make arrangements for you while I'm at work." He held out his hand to Tyler, but Tyler reflexively shoved his hands into his coat pockets.

James could have pushed the issue, insisted Tyler take his hand, physically demanded it, but what good would that do? Upsetting a five-year-old that way didn't prove a thing and somehow James had the idea that the things Tyler needed proved to him were profound and deep. "What I need from you is some co-operation. I know you don't like being here, that none of this was your idea, but right now we've got to make the best of it. Figure out what's going to make you happy…" He glanced out to the road in time to see Fallon drive by. She was headed in the direction of home, and as he watched her car wind its way down the road, the longing hit hard.

He wondered again whether he could have handled things differently after her accident. She'd needed him and he'd clearly been divided. Her needs, Tyler's needs, adjusting to fatherhood…yet he'd always thought that he could get through it and give everybody what they required. Clearly, he'd been wrong and even now, while he didn't know what it was, he was convinced Fallon had needed something he hadn't been able to give her. The hell of it was, he hadn't even realized it at the time. It was all afterthought, and filled with so many unanswered questions. But he'd been desperate back then, doing his best. Yet Fallon had insisted she understood his absences, his distractions, his moods—in short, that she was OK without him. He'd believed her, too. Trusted her. After all, Fallon was a strong woman, even with her injuries. She was a fighter, and that was something else he trusted.

But maybe he'd taken that strength too for granted, the way people in White Elk had taken her competence for granted. Maybe the brave face she'd always put on for him hadn't been so brave. And he'd never realized it. Never once questioned it.

Then the morning Shelly had taken Tyler away from him, he'd gone to Fallon's hospital room to apologize for not being there for her as much as he'd wanted. But the room had been empty, the bed stripped of its linens. There had been nothing to suggest she'd ever been there. The nurses had told him she'd gone to a rehabilitation hospital, without telling anyone which one. Or, if they knew, their loyalty to Fallon had kept them from revealing it.

Could he have done things differently? Probably. Would it have made a difference to his relationship with Fallon? That, he didn't know.

"There's someone I want you to meet," he said, glancing down at Tyler then back at Fallon's car, which was turning onto a side street. He loved Fallon, and he loved Tyler. It was time to set at least one of his mistakes right. "Look, Tyler, we're going to make a quick stop before we go to the hospital, and I need you to be on your very best behavior. Do you think you can do that for me?"

Naturally, Tyler didn't respond. All he did was follow James to the car, and crawl into the back seat after James opened the door for him. Dutifully, the little boy fastened his seat belt then he sat there like a perfect little gentleman, hands folded in his lap, staring out the window.

For a moment James studied Tyler in the rear-view mirror once he'd settled himself into the driver's seat, wondering what went on in the child's mind. Wondering what he could do to find out.

Wondering what he could do to make Tyler accept him as his father.

CHAPTER THREE

"I WANTED to see how you're doing," James said, brushing the snowflakes from his hair.

She hadn't even had time to take off her scarf. "I'm keeping busy," Fallon said, being careful to keep her back to him lest any expression of excitement or expectation accidentally crossed her face. After all, he hadn't come back to walk with her after that first time, although she'd half expected him to. Maybe even subconsciously wanted him to. He hadn't called either, and she'd half expected that. But it was probably for the best. She was working now. Not so many hours, but the progress was steady and Fallon was pleased that they were moving in the right direction to get the Three Sisters Women's Clinic and Hospital set up and staffed. It felt good to be busy again, she had to admit.

"The hospital is coming along nicely. I'm in the process of ordering room equipment right now…beds, tables, those sorts of things. And I'm beginning to go through job applications, trying to figure out what kind of staffing we'll need."

"I'd intended on stopping by sooner, maybe taking another morning walk with you. But things have gotten pretty hectic, and—"

"And that's fine. I prefer my walks in solitude." Once

though, she hadn't. "It keeps life less complicated that way."

"Maybe it does," he said, almost under his breath. "Anyway, I saw you drive by, and as I was in the area I thought I'd stop by for a minute to see how you're doing."

Finally, she turned to face him. Not that she wanted to, but she had the feeling that if she didn't, he might linger there in the doorway indefinitely…standing there, waiting for something, anything, from her. This was so awkward. She'd made love to this man. Spent nights in his arms, laughing, talking, pouring out hopes and dreams, being happier than she'd ever been in her life. *Had had his baby*. And now the only thing between them was cold, white awkwardness. It hurt, and she couldn't be anything but unapproachable. Because being anything more only encouraged him, and he deserved better than make-believe encouragement. "Look, I appreciate you coming by," she said, fixing her stare on the floor for she knew what fixing her stare on his beautiful eyes would do. "But I've got catalogs to go through, and some phone calls to—"

"Bathroom. Now!"

The tiny voice came from behind James, and Fallon immediately stepped sideways to take a look. Gasped when she saw the child. Felt her heart start to race when she noticed his startling resemblance to James.

"Now!" the little boy said. His face was deadly serious. Full of anger. An expression much too old for someone so young.

"Down the hall," she said, pointing to it. "First door."

Without a word, the child scampered out from behind James and ran down the hall, leaving a trail of slushy water and dirty snow in his wake.

"Sorry about that," James said. "I told him to stay in the car."

"When nature calls..." Fallon said, her voice not quite steady. This little boy was so much like the one she'd dreamt her own little boy would be that all the emotion she'd been fighting to hold back for so long was now fighting against her. This moment of realization unnerved her so badly that she had to back up to the wall to steady herself. This wasn't her son, she knew that. But she felt the instant connection as this was her son's brother. "I assume...assume that's Tyler?"

"Shelly dropped him off again a few days ago."

She swallowed back her emotion. She had to. There was no other way to do this with James. "A-and are you happy?" She knew he was. Happy, worried. Relieved.

"More than you can imagine. Although being his dad scares me because it's a lot of responsibility I never expected to have...at least, not right away. Not without you."

"Give it time," she said, ignoring his last comment. "The adjustment for Tyler is just as big as yours. But you'll both do fine once you're used to each other." Thinking about James and Tyler getting to know each other, working out their lives together, caused a lump to form in her throat when she thought about their child, their little boy...how they'd never have the chance to work out their lives with him. But seeing Tyler made the loss so acute again, like those first days after she'd lost her own baby. Suddenly she had to spin away from James lest he see the tears welling in her eyes. "He's cute, James," she said, walking away from the door. "I'm guessing he's, what? Five or six? You may have told me, but I don't remember."

"Five."

"And still so active?" That was a polite way of describing what James had told her early on about Tyler's behavior.

In answer to her question, a loud crash coming from the bathroom sent them both running down the hall to the open door where Tyler was standing, totally unaffected by the mess he'd made pulling a shelf of lotions and cosmetics right off the wall. And it had taken some doing, as it was hung a good three feet higher than Tyler was tall.

"He must have climbed up on the sink," Fallon said, bending to pick up a bottle of lotion. Only the bottom of the bottle had broken and when she lifted the bottle from the floor, its bottom, along with its contents, remained there, leaving Fallon holding a bottomless, empty bottle.

"Tyler," James said, his voice so quiet and controlled it was brittle.

"I'm sure it was an accident," she said, not sure what else to say, or do.

"I'm sure it was *not*," James responded.

"Maybe we should ask Tyler," Fallon said, quite surprised that he seemed totally unaffected by the whole matter. Most children his age would be scared, on the verge of tears. But Tyler had his shoulders squared, his jaw set, his arms folded belligerently across his chest. Getting ready to do battle was what Fallon immediately thought of. This child was getting ready to square off with someone. "Was it an accident, Tyler?" she asked, suddenly feeling protective of the boy.

He didn't answer. Instead, he stared straight ahead at the hall, barely blinking.

"Tyler?" she asked again.

Again, no response. She glanced up at James, who seemed in agony. Then she glanced back at Tyler, and saw just a flash of that same agony, and the need to come to his defense in some way, to make the situation a little better for him, overtook her. "Look, Tyler, I'm not going to punish you for breaking my shelf. But here's what we're going to do. I'm going to go find some rags so you can clean up the lotions and everything else that spilled on the floor. And while I'm doing that, stand back so we can get the glass picked up. We don't want you cutting yourself while you're cleaning."

"We've been having a rough time," James admitted, not so much in defense of what Tyler had done as in explanation.

"I guess you have. And it looks to me like Tyler…" Before she could finish, James's cellphone rang, and he seemed almost grateful for the interruption. Too grateful, she decided as James walked away, leaving her there to make sure Tyler didn't do something to hurt himself. Half a minute later, James returned, red-faced.

"Look, I know I don't have a right to ask this, but…I have an emergency up on Pine Ridge, a child with a broken leg, and I really can't take Tyler with me. He's…" He glanced down at the boy. "He's having a rough time right now, as you've already seen, and I don't have anyplace else for him to stay yet. He's been through three babysitters in as many days, and I haven't had time to find someone else to look after him while I'm at work. I wouldn't normally impose on you, but it may be a compound fracture, and I need to get the child stabilized before transport…"

"Just go," she said, not sure why. "Take care of your patient, and I'll look after Tyler." She glanced down at Tyler, who was eyeing another hanging shelf and trying to inch his way in its direction without being noticed. "But only for a little while."

"You don't know how much I appreciate that," James said, the expression on his face turning into genuine relief.

"We'll talk when I get back, OK? I have so much I need to tell you."

Fallon reached out and took hold of Tyler's arm to keep him from moving any closer to his next target. "When you know how long this is going to take, call me, will you?"

Instinctively, James bent to kiss Fallon's cheek, but she jerked away from him. So he simply nodded then bent to Tyler who jerked away, too. "You be good, and don't break anything else, you hear me?"

Tyler stared him in the eye, not defiantly, though. And didn't answer. After several seconds James straightened up. "Like I said, we'll talk," he said, then turned and left, leaving Fallon alone with what she knew was going to turn the rest of her day into a royal disaster.

"So, Tyler," she said, pulling him out into the hall, "tell me why you broke my shelf, and why, right this very minute, you're thinking about breaking my other shelf."

The boy's eyes opened a bit wider, as if surprised that she could anticipate what he was thinking.

Fallon laughed. "You do want to pull down the other shelf, don't you? Are you surprised that I know what you want to do?"

Naturally, he didn't respond. But that didn't surprise her. The answer was in his eyes. Big, beautiful eyes, like his father's. So beautiful she ached with longing for what she'd lost. "So I don't suppose I can trust you to stand here and not go back into the bathroom while I go find a broom to clean up the broken glass, can I?" Silly asking the question when she already knew the answer. "Which means you get to go with me." She pointed in the direction of the utility room, but Tyler kept his eyes glued to the wall across from him. What kind of trauma had done that to him? What kind of upset had caused such a young child to be so removed? James hadn't told her much. Mostly, she'd heard just the anger from him over being left out of Tyler's life, over the things he missed. Anger that sank to the heart of what she'd done to him herself, how she'd left him out, too.

And seeing Tyler, even with his problems, reminded her of how selfish she'd been. She'd made a choice that couldn't be undone. Fought hard then lost. And never included James. It was the hardest thing she'd ever done because she'd loved that baby, wanted that baby. Should have been strong enough to carry that baby to term. But she hadn't been, and the day her doctor had come to her and told her it was over...

Now she ached that their baby wasn't in her arms. "Well, Tyler," she said, trying to shake off the glum mood settling over her, "I don't know if you're hungry, but I am. And I think ice cream is a good afternoon snack. Care to have some with me?" she asked.

Naturally, Tyler didn't answer. So Fallon decided to ignore him and hope that once she got the ice cream out of the freezer, he'd come to the kitchen. Bad reasoning, though. She'd been in the kitchen less than a minute when she heard a crash. A loud crash coming from the bathroom, followed by another... "Oh, my God!" she gasped, recognizing the sound of breaking glass.

Dropping the carton of ice cream on the floor, she ran to the bathroom to find that Tyler had pulled the second cosmetic shelf down. Along with it had come a large framed picture from the wall...its glass broken into hundreds of pieces and Tyler standing in the middle of the mess, his arms and hands bleeding.

Without a thought that she, herself, could get cut, Fallon ran straight to the boy, picked him up and got him out of the bathroom. But halfway down the hall he started fighting her, kicking and screaming.

"Leave me alone!" he wailed, balling his bloody little fists and thrashing out at her. "Put me down."

"Hold still." she said, trying to have a look at the gashes on his arms without letting go of him. Which was an impossible task because Tyler was in a fit of rage, fighting her with everything he had in him. "Hold still, Tyler. I need to see how badly you're cut."

"Don't you dare!" he screamed, still fighting against her. "Just put me down or I'll…"

He didn't finish his threat but he didn't have to. Fallon knew exactly what he wanted to do, and would do the instant she let him go. So she held on even tighter, grabbed her keys from the table next to the front door, and ran as hard and as fast as she could to her car, with Tyler still pounding and kicking. Once there, she managed to get the back door open and literally had to toss him inside and get the door shut in the same swift movement. Then she locked the car with the remote control, ran to the driver's side, and simply watched Tyler for a moment. He was crying, and kicking the back of the seat. But the rage was gone, and replacing it was fear and sadness. He was now just a sad, scared little boy. Problem was, when she got in, that could change.

And it did. The instant she was behind the wheel Tyler started his tirade again, kicking the back of the seat, screaming, crying. "Tyler," she said, keeping her voice perfectly calm, "you're going to be fine. I'm a nurse, and I'm going to take you to the hospital to have your cuts taken care of." She knew that the better way would have been to stop the bleeding, remove glass fragments, bandage the wounds before moving him, but that was impossible, and her biggest fear was that in his tantrum he might injure himself further, maybe drive a glass fragment in deeper, or open a wound even more. The hospital was her only hope.

"As soon as I call your dad!"

"I don't have a dad," Tyler yelled. "Donnie didn't want me any more, and I don't want any more dads! I hate James! And I hate you!"

"He sustained some pretty good cuts." Dr. Eric Ramsey motioned Fallon into the hall. "And he was so agitated I was afraid he'd harm himself, so I had to sedate him. Just lightly. I want to keep him in for a day or so to make sure he doesn't rip out his stitches. He's…um… He's feisty. And very angry right now. I hope James will agree to let him stay for observation."

"He was so upset, Eric. I couldn't get him calmed down, and the only thing I could think of was to get him into the car and get him to the hospital. And you're right. He's a very angry little boy. But I think it's more than that. Not sure what, though."

"So you don't know anything about him?"

"James just dropped him off and, to be honest, that was the first time I'd met Tyler. I know he's been a struggle when James has had him before. But I had no idea how much."

"Well, James is en route to Salt Lake City now with his patient. It's going to be a fast turn-around, so I suppose we'll hold off making any further decisions concerning Tyler for a while." Eric was a pediatrician, and head of trauma services for the White Elk Hospital. "I've left a message to have him call here as soon as he can. So, in the meantime, we'll wait and hope Tyler calms down."

And here she was, involved. "Then I guess I'll go and

sit in Tyler's room. He'll need a familiar face there when he wakes up."

"He's going to be asleep for quite a while. How about I prescribe a cup of coffee or something to eat? And I'll get it for you myself. You're looking pretty strung out, Fallon. I don't want you letting this get to you."

"I'm feeling pretty strung out, as a matter of fact. But coffee and food aren't going to fix that." Going home and getting away from anything involving James was the prescription she needed. Only right now that prescription wasn't going to be filled because Tyler was the priority, and she felt obligated to be with him as James wasn't. More than that, she wanted to sit with him.

"Want to work?" he asked, half teasing, half serious. "I'm down a nurse today. Dinah's home with the girls. It's their regular monthly girls' day out, and she won't miss it for the world. So…"

"You know Gabby would have your head if you lured me away from her."

"And I'm still protesting that she got you and we didn't." He faked a frown. "Neil wants you back so badly that he weeps openly when your name is mentioned. You know he's at odds with his wife for stealing you away from him."

Fallon laughed, and swatted Eric's arm playfully. "I love you both, but what I'm doing right now is good. I didn't realize how much I missed being useful and for now I like the job." Not the way she liked real nursing. But for a while, until she figured out what she really wanted to do with her life, it would do.

"Well, I'm glad you're back, even if it's with Gabby," he admitted, laughing.

Fallon looked down the hall of the trauma area and sighed. Yes, Gabby did have her. And she was grateful for that. Which meant White Elk Hospital was officially the past now. If only she could return to the past and stay there for ever.

"How is he?" James gasped, running through the door. "I just got the message. I was on my way back when I remembered to check my voicemail."

"Resting," Fallon said. She'd been sitting at Tyler's bedside well over an hour, simply watching the boy. He was even troubled in his sleep. She could see that in the way he tossed and turned and twisted in his covers. "Eric gave him a light sedative and I didn't want to leave him so I've been sitting here for a while, and he's doing well." Physically well, anyway. She wasn't sure about anything else.

"The cuts are all superficial," Eric said, stepping into the room. "He has a few stitches, and he's good to go as far as his injuries are concerned. But I'd like to keep him under observation for a while because he was so…I suppose the word to describe it is enraged. He was having a major temper tantrum when Fallon brought him in, fighting her as hard as he could, and I was afraid he'd hurt himself so I gave him something to take the edge off a little, and now I'd like to watch him for a day or so to see if there's anything else wrong with him other than his cuts."

James agreed quickly. "I wish I knew his history…if he's always like this or if this is new behavior. Because it's extreme. Children have their temper tantrums and that's part of learning how to cope with disappointment, but when I see a child like Tyler, who acts it out so violently, I'm inclined to look for something other than the momentary trigger of those emotions. I've had him three days this time and he's getting worse, so I think observing him for a day or two, running some tests to make sure he doesn't have some underlying medical problem, is a good idea. I appreciate the offer, and I'd appreciate it if you'd oversee his care, Eric."

"Look," Eric said, "I've got to get back to work. But, yes, James, I'll take over his medical treatment, observe him, run some preliminary tests. You know, blood tests, a general physical, maybe some X-rays, that sort of thing. So, until we know more, if you have any questions, call me. And feel free to sit with Tyler for as long as you like. I'm sure he'll be happy to have you with him when he wakes up."

"I'm not so sure of that," James muttered, slumping to the wall as Eric took his leave. "I'm really sorry about all this, Fallon. I didn't mean to drag you into it. This whole thing with Tyler has been...difficult."

"Have you talked to his mother about how he's acting? Maybe she knows what triggers the temper tantrums."

"Do you think she'd actually tell me anything? I mean, she didn't even tell me I had a son until her husband didn't want him any more. If Tyler had been a well-behaved child, I'm pretty sure she would have never revealed her little *secret* about his existence. So I have no reason to believe that she'll tell me anything about his behavior. The hell of it is, Fallon, that when she drops him off and leaves, I don't even know where she goes. Don't know where Tyler lives when he's not with me. They have a son of their own now, and Donnie, the husband, doesn't want Tyler around. I'd wanted to ask her some questions, so a couple of months ago, after she disappeared with Tyler for the second time, I hired an investigator to find them. But apparently she and Donnie move around a lot, and every time my investigator catches up to her, she moves again. So we start over." He sucked in a sharp, angry breath.

"Secrets. Her stupid damn secrets are killing me, and I can't do a thing about it."

Secrets… Reality sprouted in the form of a dull ache in her chest. "But you're going after custody?"

He nodded. "My first round didn't turn out so well. I didn't have the results of the DNA test back, although our blood types matched. And the judge wouldn't hear the case. To make matters worse, Shelly came back in the middle of that mess and wanted Tyler back, and the judge said I had no legal recourse at that point, that I had to let Tyler go. So I did, then I couldn't find him again."

"It must be awful for both of you, never knowing what she's going to do."

"This time it may not be up to Shelly to decide."

It was unthinkable, what Tyler's mother was doing to him. What she was doing to James. Poor child. Poor James. "And nothing's getting better yet, is it?"

He shook his head. "Tyler's so angry, and he's frightened, and I can't blame him. When I grew up I had great parents who took care of me, protected me. At his age, I probably had no concept that one, or both, of my parents could simply get rid of me the way Shelly did Tyler. I can't even imagine…"

"Well, however it works out in the long run, you have Tyler right now and I know you'll do whatever's best for him. And if there's anything I can do in the meantime to help him…"

"Actually, if you ever run onto a place where Tyler and I can live…"

"Where are you now?"

"We're staying in a hotel room. One room, with a microwave and a mini-fridge. Two beds, a television and a lamp. For me, it was fine. I wasn't in a hurry to find a house or a condo because this is the tourist season and

I know nothing's available. But the thing is, I won't get custody of Tyler if I don't have a stable home for him. And that little room isn't enough for him. He's bouncing off the walls, it's driving him crazy. So if you know of a place I can rent, or even buy... Oh, and a care-giver, too. As of this morning Tyler has exhausted the list of available care-givers in the area...at least, the ones with a recommendation from the hospital pediatric department. I'm pretty sure his reputation precedes him now, which will make the possibility of finding someone else to care for him while I'm working slim to none. So if you know someone who's up to a challenge..."

"Let me think about it. Make some calls, see if I can figure something out for you...for Tyler."

"It's not your problem, but I'd appreciate it." Stepping away from the wall, James bent and gave Fallon a quick kiss on the cheek, one from which she didn't flinch this time. "I'm sorry for so many things, Fallon. But I haven't had a lot of options lately."

"I know," she whispered, trying to push back the emotions straining to spring up in her. It was hard thinking of James and Tyler struggling so much. "And you did the right thing then. Still are. So, let me know how he gets along," she said. "Because I do care." He was her son's brother, how could she not care? "And in the meantime, if I can find you and Tyler a place to live..." Spinning away, too full of emotion and her own regrets to be near James any longer, Fallon had every intention of dashing for the exit, which was exactly what she did. But something tugged at her halfway there. It was an image of James and Tyler living in a small hotel room, an image of the judge taking Tyler away from James because James couldn't provide a proper home. It wasn't fair! But, then, life wasn't fair, was it? If it were, she and James and Tyler would be living together now, with the baby. The four of them as a family. Yet James and Tyler were stuck in a cramped hotel room and there was no way a judge would grant James the sole custody he wanted. And Tyler...he really did need a home, needed to be with James as much as James needed to be with his son. *The way she so longed to be with her own son.*

She understood that need in such deep, agonizing ways now, and it was causing the sprout of a plan to grow. One that sprouted then grew so rapidly it surprised her.

But could she do it? Could she take James and Tyler into her home temporarily? Give them the stability they needed, the stability the judge would demand? Could she do that and keep herself separated from them?

She shut her eyes, trying to fight off the plan. It was ridiculous, and James was right. It wasn't her problem. Yet behind her shut eyes she saw Tyler, looking so alone and frightened. Tyler without a home. Saw the judge pulling Tyler away from James. Saw the judge sending her son's brother back to a terrible home. That was the vision that turned her around and sent her right back to James.

"James," she said quietly, on entering the hospital room where Tyler was still sleeping peacefully. "I've been thinking. It's not good to keep Tyler in a hotel room. He needs a home, someplace where he's going to feel safe. Someplace where he can live a normal life, where the judge can see stability. Since you can't find that right now, I think you two should come and stay at my cabin. It's not large, but I have a spare bedroom, plenty of space for a little boy. *For a little while.* There's a nice hill out back where he can sled and play in the snow.

"I mean, I realize it's not going to solve all his problems, or yours, but maybe it will help make things a little better in the meantime. And we can work out our schedules to watch him so he'll have some kind of consistency in his life, and you won't have to worry about finding someone else to look after him. I'm at home most of the time with my new job…at least, for now. And you can work your shifts around what I need to do. Eric and Neil are all into family these days, and I'm pretty sure that's what they'd want you to do."

"Why would you do that, Fallon?" James whispered, stepping quietly away from the bed, trying not to disturb the boy. "Considering the way we are now, why would you take us in?"

Because Tyler was lost, and she knew how that felt. Because James was at a confusing, frustrating place in his life and she knew how *that* felt. Because Tyler was so connected to her son. "Don't ask me personal questions," she said. "I'm not getting involved with you again. This is only a temporary solution to a bigger problem, *your problem*, and I don't want you getting any other ideas about anything. *Especially about us.* That's the only condition. Tyler gets the spare bedroom, you get the couch, and you both respect my privacy."

James looked down at Tyler then turned back to Fallon. "Do you really think he looks like me? People tell me he does."

Too much so, she thought. Because she was well on her way to losing her heart to the son, like she'd already done to the father. This wasn't good. Not good at all. But it wasn't about her, wasn't even about James. It was about Tyler. And as long as she kept that in mind, she'd be fine. "He does look like you." The way she thought their son would have.

CHAPTER FOUR

"WHAT was I thinking?" Fallon was exhausted from sheer worry by the time the end of the day rolled around. Intermittently, she was positive she'd done the right thing, allowing James and his son to move in temporarily with her. Then she was positive it was the worst thing she could have done. Back and forth, all day long. That, mixed with cold chills, shaking hands and throbbing head. For heaven's sake! After so many months fighting to be alone, she'd just gone and done the very last thing she'd wanted to do. "How could I have invited them?" she moaned on a weary sigh. Yet how could she have not done that? The bigger question, though, was how could she live with them and still remain disengaged from their lives?

She was already becoming engaged, especially with Tyler, and that was the problem. A huge problem because he wasn't her son. Wasn't a replacement for her son. Yet she had these motherly feelings toward him, feelings she couldn't have because she and James had no future together.

"It's a good deed, the right thing to do," she said, hoping that saying it aloud would convince her. "The thing any normal, decent person would do." No personal involvement permitted. "Good deed, good deed…" Besides, they wouldn't be staying long. "Good deed, Fallon. That's all it is."

The personal pep talk kept up as she prepared the bedroom for Tyler and the couch for James. No physical contact with James. No hugs, no kisses, no nothing. That, more than anything, was going to be the tough part, because there was no denying that she still craved his touch, his kiss. Craved every inch of him in a way she'd never known one person could crave another. "It's *just* a good deed…"

She *had* to keep her head about this. Because, maybe, just maybe, helping him through this rough patch would assuage some of her guilt. Or make it ever stronger.

Nevertheless, she was petrified that one little look from James could undo everything—her resolve, her resistance, both of them flying right out the window. Fighting against everything she'd hoped for in a life with James was the hardest thing she'd ever done. So she had to brace herself for that fight. Had to convince herself she was going to win it. Had to remind herself that she was doing this for James.

"Good deed," she said, heading to the kitchen to fix herself a cup of hot tea. "If I don't let my emotions get the better of me." Because she'd never stopped loving James, and she truly did care what happened to Tyler. Because she wasn't strong enough to completely divorce herself from the things she'd thought, for a time, she'd have in her life—the things she'd always wanted. Husband, children… "Because I'm crazy," she was repeating as someone rang the doorbell. At the same time her cellphone also jingled its Beethoven sonata. "Hello," she said, on her way to the front door.

"It's me. I didn't want to alarm you so after I knocked I called to tell you that I'm here with my things."

He was moving in tonight? Suddenly the thing she wanted, and dreaded, was happening, and she was a nervous wreck.

"Why now?" she said in wobbly greeting when she pulled open the door.

"Why not now?"

"Because I thought you'd move in once Tyler was released from the hospital."

"But I'm not working now, not on call, so I thought this was as good a time as any. Unless you don't want me yet, then I can..."

"What? Sleep in your car outside my house?"

Grinning, he looked almost as innocent as a young schoolboy. "Or bunk at the hospital in one of the on-call rooms until you're ready for us."

Why was it that just one smile was all it took and she was done for? "You don't have to spend your night in an on-call room."

"Then I can move in here, or is it back to the car?"

Now he was teasing her. She could see it in his eyes, in the way he couldn't keep a straight face even though he tried. Her old feelings were pummeling her now, and she had to duck her head to hide her feelings from James. Because what she could read in his eyes, he could read in hers. That's what had connected them initially. One look, she saw his soul. And he saw hers. "In here. I probably should send you back to the car, though," she said, trying to sound grumpy.

"Then I'll be right back." After dropping a duffle bag on the entry hall floor, he headed back out to his car then returned almost immediately with a couple of suitcases. "This is all I've got. Didn't bring any of the things with me from my apartment when I came here. Just a few clothes and some medical journals."

"What about Tyler's things?"

James shook his head. "Shelly didn't leave anything for him. I bought him a few clothes to wear, but I haven't had time to do much shopping for him yet. And he wasn't exactly easy to take to the department store the one time I did try. Let's just say that he was too exuberant with his opinion and we were kicked out within twenty minutes."

"Maybe I'll take him shopping when he's up to it. If that's OK with you."

"Oh, it's OK. I'd be grateful."

So there it was. One minute into the arrangement, resolve already flying away. She was getting involved. But it was with Tyler. Not James. That's what she had to tell herself. *It was for Tyler.*

Fallon stepped back as James walked fully into her house then she shut the door behind him. "You can have the spare room until Tyler moves in. It's down the hall, near the back. Bathroom is...well, you know where that is. And when Tyler's here you can have the couch in the living room, or there's one in the den. It's not as large, but you can shut the door and have your privacy. Take your pick. I'm upstairs, by the way, and there's no reason for you to come up there. My office is behind the stairs on this floor, so while you're here, it's your responsibility to see that Tyler stays out." She sounded like a cranky landlady all of a sudden, and it was all she could to do bite back a smile. Truth was, she'd rehearsed those words a few times. Out loud. Trying to sound churlish when she said them. She'd succeeded and she was a little proud of herself for it...proud that a little of that resolve was flying back through the window.

"Shall I have security bars installed at the bottom of the stairway?" James teased. "And another on your bedroom door?"

OK, so maybe she hadn't sounded as churlish as she'd wanted to. Resolve flying back out again. Then, to make matters worse, he didn't even try biting back his smile. It was broad, and so infectious Fallon glanced away so he wouldn't see the corners of her lips turning up. He always did that, always cured her disagreeable moods with a simple smile.

"Are you smiling, Fallon?" he asked.

"No," she lied.

"Can I see?"

"No."

"If I can't have a look, I have to presume that you're smiling."

"I don't smile."

"If you don't, it's a pity, because you have the most beautiful smile in the world."

She raised her head to look at him. "Flattery's not going to get you to the top of the stairs, James, if that's what you're trying to do here."

"I didn't think it would. And so you'll know, Fallon, I won't take one step up those stairs unless you want me to. The only thing that will get me to the top will be your invitation, and you have my word on that."

"Thank you," she whispered.

"It's not what I want, and you know that." Instinctively, he reached out, placed his fingers gently under her chin and raised her face to him even more. "I love you, and it's not going to be easy on me living here, knowing that you won't have me. But I'll respect your wishes. And your boundaries. Even if I don't agree with them."

"Thank you," she said again, fighting the urge to cry. He was so kind and good, and so…chivalrous. In time, after she'd pushed him away enough, he would realize he didn't want her any more. But for now he was being a perfect gentleman. Yet, God willing, if she could push hard enough, it would wear thin on him. Pray that day came quickly because, try as she may, she would slip. Sooner or later, she'd give in to that smile, to those twinkling eyes. Then she'd tell him her awful secret. And hurt him in ways she couldn't even imagine. "Look, I was about to fix myself a cup of tea. Would you care to join me?"

"Are you sure you want me here?" he asked, quite seriously. "I know you asked because that's just the thing you'd do. But do you really want me...*us*—here?"

"I wasn't sure about it when I asked you, and nothing's changed. But I'm not going back on my invitation. Tyler needs something other than a hotel room, and—"

"This arrangement is *only* about Tyler?" he asked, trying to sound neutral.

But Fallon heard no neutrality there...only hope, as she looked him square in the eye. "This is *only* about Tyler. I know what it's like to be...abandoned. That's what happened to me. My mother had me, didn't want me, passed me off to anybody who wanted to be charitable for a while and take me in. So I know why he needs stability, especially for Christmas."

"I'm so sorry, Fallon," he whispered, reaching out to stroke her cheek. "I didn't know that about you. You'd never told me, and you should have."

So many things she hadn't told him. She lurched back. "Don't do that, James. I just...I just can't deal with it." For a moment, she thought about taking his single room at the lodge. Shutting herself in with the microwave and mini-fridge. It wouldn't be so bad for a while, and she wouldn't have to deal with this. But James needed help with Tyler, and part of having them live there was that help. Truth was, she wanted to help. Tyler really did need that stability. "Look, I think I'm going to go upstairs for a while. Help yourself to anything you need, feel free to make yourself at home, kick around, open cupboards, get yourself familiar with what's here. Shout if you need something you can't find."

"I'm not sorry I touched you, Fallon. I'll respect the boundaries from now on, like I promised, but I'm not sorry."

"You're going to make this difficult for me, aren't you?"

"It's not my intention. But you know what? It's difficult on me, too. You know how I feel about you, but what you don't know is how I feel every time you push me away. It's killing me."

She thrust her hand to stop him. "Don't!" she said. "Don't tell me. Don't tell me…anything, because I don't want to know." Miserably, she already knew, but what James didn't fathom was how each time she pushed him away a tiny piece of her heart broke off. She was losing herself, one shred at a time, and the pain of it was unrelenting. It was a wound that would not heal. Not ever. And, she'd never show it to him. Because once he saw the weakness, he'd find his way in.

Stretching out on the couch in the den, James stared up at the ceiling, wondering if her bed was above him. He imagined that it was, and that she was sleeping there. He loved the way she slept…on her side, cuddled into a little ball. He remembered their first night together when he'd stayed awake hours, just watching her. He'd been tempted to disturb her, just to see if she would cuddle into him, but he hadn't. Second night, she'd cuddled into him, and he'd thought that was the way he wanted to spend every night for the rest of his life. "And we will, Fallon," he promised himself. "But I've got to find a way to convince you that you want it as much as I do."

Working on that solution was cut short by a phone call, though. It was Neil Ranard, informing him that every available medic in the White Elk Valley was being called out. The lodge on the Little Sister was on fire! Grease fire in the kitchen, spreading.

"Fallon!" James yelled, jumping up from the couch. "Medical emergency! Neil says he needs your help!"

She was down the stairs in a flash, blanket wrapped around her shoulders. "What?" she gasped.

"Fire. Lodge up on the Little Sister. He wants you in the ER, in charge of triage. Wants me in the ER, too."

Surprisingly, she didn't protest, didn't even think about it. Instead, she dropped the blanket to the floor and headed back to the stairs. "Give me three minutes to get ready," she called back over her shoulder on her way up. James could hear her footsteps pounding on the wooden floor-boards upstairs. That was Fallon O'Gara preparing to do what she'd been put on this earth to do—be a nurse. It was a good sound to hear. Gave him hope for other things. Made him glad to know that Fallon wouldn't turn away when she was needed.

It was a good sign, seeing how the woman he'd come to love so quickly didn't turn away when she was needed. Except from him. Sadly, she'd found that easy to do.

Fifteen minutes after the initial callout, James and Fallon crashed through the emergency room doors together, shoulder to shoulder, and ran straight into a wall of vol-unteers and medical personnel alike. People Fallon knew, people who always responded when there was a need. People waiting for her instructions.

"How many doctors do we have?" she asked Emoline Putters, the night clerk in charge of the emergency desk.

"Two, so far. Dr. Galbraith and Dr. Ranard...Gabby.

She's on her way in as soon as Angela Blanchard gets there to look after Bryce. She'll be on light duty, considering her condition. Walt Graham may be heading into town, too. And Henry Gunther." A retired obstetrician and a semi-retired anesthesiologist.

"Dr. Eric Ramsey isn't here?"

Emoline, a tight-faced woman with gray- and brown-streaked hair pulled into a knot at the nape of her neck, shook her head. "He went out with Dr. Neil Ranard. First time back on the rescue for him. Dr. McGinnis went out with him, too. I've been trying to locate Dr. Stafford to come in, but so far he isn't answering his cellphone."

Fallon spun to face James. "How much experience do you have with treating burns?" she asked. It was a difficult specialty, took stamina. In her opinion, burns were the worst of the worst to tend, and she never assigned anyone to burns unless they had the experience. Some of the doctors who passed through here wouldn't treat burns unless absolutely forced to.

"I worked in the pediatric side of the burn unit back in Salt Lake City," he said. "I'm not a burn specialist by a long shot, but I can do the initial assessments and stabilize them. Get them ready to transport to a burn unit."

"Well, we're not set up with a specific burn room, but exam five is larger, probably the best one." She motioned for one of the volunteers to come over. Dave Ellis, the town dentist. "Dave, you go with Dr. Galbraith, and get the room ready. He'll tell you what he needs. You can hang the IVs and get the saline ready." She also signaled Catie, the owner of Catie's Overlook, to help. Catie would fetch, Dave would actually assume some of the medical duty.

"Who are these people?" James whispered to her.

"They're not trained to do the actual rescue out in the field, but I've trained them to help in the ER—they run errands, go after supplies, carry messages, do whatever they can to help the medical staff. In the case of Dave Ellis, he's got a fair amount of medical training as he's a dentist, and he can do pretty much anything we need him to."

"Amazing," he said, looking around at the expanding sea of these volunteers. At least fifteen of them had wandered in now.

"Yes, they are," she said, taking some pride in her little group.

"Not them. You. They're here because of you, aren't they?"

She looked up at him. Smiled. For a moment, an old longing filled her. She wanted to feel his arms around her, just a fleeting hug, but she stepped back before he saw the need reflected in her eyes. And he would. "They're here because this is where they want to be. It has nothing to do with me."

"I don't believe that," James argued. "Just look at the way they're watching you, waiting for instructions."

They were waiting for her and it was nice to be back. A little bit of normalcy in the midst of so many things that hadn't been normal for so long. "Honestly, I'm a little nervous," she whispered to him. "It's been a while…not sure I'll get my old rhythm back."

"Smoke inhalation coming in…times three, ETA ten minutes," Emoline shouted. "One critical, two stable."

"You're going to be fine," James whispered, his lips practically brushing her ear. "It's like riding a bicycle. You may not have been on one in a while, but once you get back on…"

She felt the tingle of his lips on her ear. It spread down her neck, down her arms, down to her toes. "Running an

emergency is like riding a bicycle?" she asked, fighting
not to visibly shiver.

"OK, so maybe the analogy was a little off, but you
know what I mean."

"Yes," she whispered. "I do. And thank you for having
that confidence in me."

"I know who you are. And usually I might say something like, if you need me, you know where I am. But I
don't have to say that, Fallon, because you *won't* need
me."

That wasn't true. She'd needed him from the first
moment she'd laid eyes on him. That would never change.
For her, James was everything, and her need for him was
so close to the surface it was nearly touchable.

"Burn coming in, ETA twenty minutes. They're telling
me it's minor," Emoline called out.

Fallon drew in a deep breath. Smiled at James, reached
out and gave his hand a squeeze. "I'm glad you're here
tonight," she said, then turned to the group. "OK, I need
two of you at the door to keep it clear..." She gave the
instructions, volunteers scurried to obey, and within mere
minutes the emergency room was ready. A short time later,
while she was awaiting the arrival of Gabby Ranard,
who was going to be doctor in charge, her dear old friend
Edith Weston staggered into the emergency room on her
own, looking ashen, confused. "Don't feel good...called
a taxi..." The rest of her words were garbled as Fallon
rushed forward to grab her when the old woman started
to pitch forward.

One of the volunteers was there right away with a
wheelchair, helping Edith into it. Fallon assessed her
pupils immediately, took a pulse after that. "Edith, can
you tell me what happened?"

Edith looked up at her, flashed confusion. "I think I

may have had a slight stroke, dear. When the fire started, I was gathering up my photo albums, hurrying too much, then…" She shook her head. "I don't remember." Edith Weston lived at the lodge. Was one of White Elk's grand matriarchs.

"We're going to get you comfortable, Edith. Are you in any pain?"

The woman shook her head. "Just embarrassed that I'm taking up your time when you have so much to do."

Fallon patted her hand. "Truth is, Edith, I'd rather have you taking up my time than anyone else."

"I'm still sorry about my timing," Edith managed. She reached out and took hold of Fallon's hand. "But my home is burning down now, so I guess this is as good a place for me as any."

Edith was showing such courage in the face of adversity. It was something Fallon wished for herself, but her time for that kind of courage had passed, and she'd proved herself lacking. "Did you get your photo albums?" Fallon asked. "Before you had to leave, were you able to find them?"

"Most of them. The important ones. One of the firefighters put them aside for me, promised he'd bring them to the hospital for me later. Those are my memories, Fallon. Good and bad, memories are the things we can hold dear when everything else is gone."

"Well, I'll make sure they get to your room. And, Edith, if you need anything…*anything*…please let me know." Edith was like the grandmother she'd never had. The one who'd baked her cookies over the years, and listened to her when everything had been falling apart. Edith had come to sit with her in the rehabilitation hospital, the only person she'd asked to be there while fighting for her life at first, then fighting to keep her baby. She hadn't included Gabby or Dinah, hadn't included James. But she'd turned to Edith because she'd needed the comfort of a mother or grandmother. Someone who'd seen life and known its pain. Someone whose sympathy was expressed in her eyes, and by the way she'd held Fallon's hand in the roughest hours. Her other friends would have cried, their eyes would have been sad. But what Edith had given her had been poised composure at a time when that's what she'd needed more than anything. "But right now we need to get you into bed and make sure you're as comfortable as possible. Then get a doctor in to see you."

Edith looked up at Fallon and there were no lies to be told in the eyes of either woman. "I worry about you, Fallon. When I knew *he* was here… You're not making it right between you two yet, are you? You haven't told him the things he has a right to know?"

"And hurt him?"

"Pain is part of life, my dear. Once in a while it makes us grow stronger. Often, when it's shared with those we love, we become better for it."

"I made bad choices, Edith. You know that. You were there, telling me to do the right thing. And I wasn't listening to you."

"But it's never too late to do the right thing, dear. Never too late."

Down the hall, James watched the exchange between the two women. While he couldn't hear what they were saying, he saw the tender, caring way Fallon responded to the woman in the wheelchair, and he wanted to punch the wall in frustration. Tomorrow, when this was over, she would go right back to being the way she'd been all these months, withdrawn, hesitant. At least, with him. And it was so wrong. Yet he wasn't sure he knew how to get through to her…not in the way that mattered. As more nurses showed up to work, and a few more doctors came in as well, all of them glad to take instruction from Fallon, all of them depending on her to make the emergency room work the way it should, James knew, more than ever, that he couldn't give up on Fallon. He wasn't sure he could fix *their* relationship, wasn't sure they could ever get back to the place they'd been before she'd been injured. But he was sure that Fallon needed this hospital and, more than that, this hospital needed Fallon.

So did he. But would they work things out between them? Would he get her back? Because Fallon had changed in ways he didn't understand, ways she wouldn't share with him. It scared him, because he wasn't sure what to do any more. Wasn't sure he'd ever be let back in.

CHAPTER FIVE

BY ALL estimations, James still had a few minutes before the first patients would arrive...enough time to dash down to the pediatrics ward to check on Tyler. So he let Fallon know where to find him and hurried down the hall to his room.

"Tyler," James said, entering the ward. "Are you feeling better?"

The boy was sitting cross-legged in the middle of the bed with a game controller in his hand. His attention was totally fixed on a game...something with colorful little animals scurrying in and out of little holes in the ground. He didn't so much as blink when James entered the room. But, then, James was used to that reaction. Understood it, didn't like it but was braced for it.

"Looks like a fun game," James continued, grappling for words as the level of discomfort started to germinate. Funny how he was always so good with other people's children, yet with his own... "Are you winning?"

Tyler shot him a dark scowl, as if James should know that. Wasn't a great response, but it was a response.

"I've never really played any video games before, but I wouldn't mind trying. Can that one be played by two people?"

"I don't want to play with anyone," Tyler said, his tiny

voice defiant. As if he wanted to prove that point, he scooted to the far edge of the bed, as far away from James as he could possibly get.

James chose not to react. Instead, he sat down next to the bed, stretched out his long legs, and relaxed back into the chair. "Why don't you show me how to play," he said, "in case I ever want to try it? Tell me what to do, show me where all those animals are supposed to go." He didn't have time for this, but he couldn't just walk away from Tyler and leave him here alone in such a defensive mood.

Tyler cast a suspicious glance at James out of the corner of his eye, but didn't refuse. Good step, James decided. Small one, but one that seemed headed in the right direction.

"You have to get the red bunnies in the biggest holes with their mommies…that's where they live. And the green squirrels up in the trees 'cause that's where they live with their mommies. And the baby bears have to go in the caves with their mommies so they're safe for the night, 'cause if you don't get them in before the moon comes out, they have to stay outside. But if you do get them all in before the moon, the moon comes out faster next time. And their houses move around."

"Is it bad if they have to stay out all night?" James asked, impressed by Tyler's command of the game.

"They get cold, and scared."

That wasn't in the game, of course, but for James the simple explanation proved what he'd suspected…Tyler was bright. And much more aware of his surroundings than he let on. "Would the mommies miss them if they had to stay out all night?"

A flash of hurt crossed Tyler's face, coming and going so fast that if James hadn't been watching for a reaction he would have missed it. "The mommies don't care," he said. "They have other little boys...bunnies and squirrels and baby bears to take care of."

"But would they miss their mommies?"

Tyler didn't answer that one. Rather, he turned his full attention to the game, clicking the controls like a child possessed. Soon he would have to have that serious talk with Tyler. The child deserved to know. "Look, I've got to get back to work. You do know what I do, don't you?"

Tyler shrugged.

Not to be daunted, James persisted. "I take care of sick people."

"Am I sick?" Tyler asked, keeping his gaze steady on the television screen even though, for the moment, he'd stopped playing. "Is that why my mommy always brings me to you? 'Cause I'm sick, and you're a doctor?"

It didn't get easier for the child. Or for James. "No, you're not sick. Except for your cuts and scrapes, you're in very good health. And remember last time we were together, when I told you I was your dad?"

"Donnie was my dad, too. But not any more. I like doctors better than dads!"

It was so hard, not telling him he wanted full custody. But what happened if he told Tyler, and Tyler counted on that, then the courts didn't comply? What happened if Shelly took him back yet again? "Look, Tyler, I've got to work now, but I'll check on you later. And, Tyler..." He handed the boy a slip of paper with his cellphone number written on it. "If you need to talk to me, call. You do know how to use a phone, don't you?"

Tyler didn't answer, but he did put the paper under his pillow. Then he scooted back to the middle of the bed, resumed his cross-legged position, and totally blocked James out.

"I'll be back when I can, Tyler," James said on his way out the door. But as usual Tyler didn't respond. All he did was turn up the volume of the game and click away on the control as fast as his little fingers would move.

Everything that could be made ready had been by the time the first patients began to be wheeled into the emergency department. Three burns cases went straight to James and a couple of smoke inhalations were assigned to Gabby, as well as a sprained ankle...someone falling down the stairs, trying to escape. "You OK?" Fallon asked, poking her head into the makeshift burn unit. James was busy with the worst of his patients, getting oxygen started on the man, a belligerent patient who was fighting James every step of the way. Dave Ellis was busy treating minor burns on the other two, who turned out to be kitchen workers at the lodge, while Catie, the volunteer, was setting up the supplies being called for by both Dave and James.

Immediately Fallon rushed into the room to help subdue the patient, who calmed down immediately when he saw who she was. She gave James a quick acknowledgment then pulled the IV set-up to the bedside. "You'll be fine, Mr. Chambers. You've got some serious burns to your chest, but once I can get the IV in, we'll get some pain medicine going and you'll feel much better."

"I've heard how bad burns can be, Miss O'Gara," the man managed from behind his oxygen mask.

"They can be, and I won't lie to you. Your chest and left shoulder look fairly involved, but it's a relatively small area. We're going to treat you here then send you to a burn unit in Salt Lake City, and you're going to be fine."

"Thank you," he whispered, fighting back tears.

She glanced over at James, who was busy cooling down the burns with saline. "Mr. Chambers is the caretaker at the lodge," she explained, as she squeezed the frightened man's hand. "His granddaughter is going to be a nurse."

"Like Miss O'Gara," the man said. "She helped Allison with her application to nursing school, let her work part time at the hospital after school, and even gave her a personal recommendation."

"Because she deserved it." Fallon deflected the direction of the conversation with a blush. "Look, I'll check back in on you before you go," she told him, then turned her attention on James. "Are you good here? I'd like to check in on Edith, if you don't need me…"

"Go," he said. "We're good."

Fallon was halfway to the hall when James caught up with her. "Are you OK?" he asked, taking hold of her arm to stop her. "You're running circles around everybody here."

"It's what I do…"

"Maybe it's what you do, but I'm concerned about you. It's going to be a long night, and you haven't done this for a while."

She bristled immediately. "You think I can't?"

"Oh, I'm sure you can. But you worry me."

"Well, I'm not yours to worry about, am I?" she said, jerking her arm away from him.

"That's not going to stop me from worrying, Fallon. One minute you don't ever want to step foot in the emergency department again, and the next you're working like a woman possessed. I understand the dynamics here. Everybody depends on you…the staff, the volunteers, even the patients. But what about you? Who do you depend on, especially when everything's going crazy the way it is?"

"I depend on me," she whispered. "Look, I appreciate your concern, but I got along fine before…" Before the accident, before James. Before so many things in her life had changed in ways she hated.

"Before me?" he asked.

"Yes," she said, trying to be defiant about it. But there was no defiance in her. "This is what I've always done, it's who I am." Rather, who she'd once been, and who she wanted to be again. Right now, she was play-acting her way through it, but someday, maybe…

"Not who you are, Fallon," he said, raising his hand to brush her cheek. "It's only a small part of you. There's so much more. So many things I'm not sure you even see."

For an instant she didn't flinch, it was as if she'd forgotten she was supposed to. Then, suddenly, she did. Flinched, pulled back. Cleared her throat to throw off the tension. "Look, Emoline will call for transport when you're ready to send Mr. Chambers to the burn unit. And I need to—"

"Don't overdo it, Fallon. That's all I'm saying. If you need help, you know where I am. Just ask me, will you?"

Just ask… So hard to do, because she wanted to separate from James, not draw closer or become more dependent. Except her heart wanted to meld so badly with his…

"Edith," she said, stepping into the quiet room a minute or two later. It was well away from all the activity, its window with a lovely view of the Older Sister. Safety for a moment. Away from James. "How are you feeling?" she asked, pulling up a chair to the old lady's bedside.

"I know you have more important things to do than sit with me," the woman said.

"There's nothing more important than sitting here with you for a few moments. And if anybody needs me, they know where I am."

"It's so good to see you working again. It's not too much for you, is it?"

"They need me, and I'm doing fine."

"Or you need them. Because you do need this, Fallon." Edith turned her head to the window. "It's a lovely sight," she said, "and I think it's true what they say about the Three Sisters protecting everyone in their shadows. I've lived a blessed life here. Wouldn't have changed a thing about it."

"It's an amazing place," Fallon agreed. "I missed it when I wasn't here." Wanted to get home. Ached to get home. "It was good to get back."

"Good to have you back," Edith choked out. "But you don't look happy, dear."

"I'm fine," she said. "It's been difficult, but I'm getting better."

"No, I don't think you are. Fine is OK, happy is better. You need to be happy again. The way you used to be. You don't smile now, and I miss that."

If only it was that simple. "I'm building up to...well, my old life, I suppose."

"You're blocking it out," Edith argued, then smiled. "Stubbornness. Good when you use it wisely, bad when you use it against yourself. And that's what you're doing, you know. You're denying what you want. Denying *that* you want."

"Can I get you something to drink, Edith? Some tea, or juice?"

"Ignoring it won't make it go away, Fallon."

"Where were you all those years when I needed a mother?"

Edith laughed. "You still need a mother, dear. We all do sometimes. And mothers come in so many forms, don't they?" She turned her head to the window. "Isn't it beautiful? I want to see the view while I still can." She drew in a wistful breath. "You need to see the whole view, Fallon. That's where you'll find your happiness." Her eyes started to flutter shut. "I promise, that's where you'll find it, *when* you want it badly enough."

Fallon pulled the sheet over Edith's shoulder and gave her a gentle kiss on the cheek. "It used to be a lovely view, Edith. But I can't bear looking at it any more."

"Stubborn," Edith whispered, although her eyes were closed. "That's all it is."

The hallway wall outside Edith's door turned out to be a great support as Fallon leaned heavily against it for a moment, thinking about the woman's words. *You need to see the whole view, Fallon. That's where you'll find your happiness.* The whole view…whatever that was. She wasn't sure she would want to see it even if she knew what it was.

Shutting her eyes, Fallon rubbed her head, bracing herself to go back to the emergency department. It was a stressful, busy night. She wanted it to be over, wanted the morning to dawn bright and sunny, wanted everything to be right. But she knew better. Practical experience was always the best teacher. And usually the harshest.

Harsh… She peeked into Tyler's room on her way back to Emergency. Harsh shouldn't have any place in the life of a child but sadly it did all too often. Poor Tyler was only at the beginning of what was going to be harsh in his world, and she wasn't sure there was any way around it. James would help him, though. He'd be an amazing father… *was* an amazing father. Someone who deserved to be an amazing father to other children. "You OK?" she asked from the doorway. Tyler was sitting on the bed, playing a video game.

"Fine," he said, his voice so quiet she barely heard him.

"You winning?"

He shrugged.

"Look, we're really busy in Emergency right now. But how about I come see you later, when things slow down?"

He shrugged again, and Fallon turned to leave. But before she had stepped away from the door, Tyler spoke up.

"Why?" he asked.

"Why what?"

"Why are you busy?"

"There was a big fire tonight at one of the buildings up on the mountain. If anybody gets hurt, we have to take care of them."

"I didn't do it!" he said, dropping his game controller and scurrying for the shelter of his blankets. "I didn't start the fire."

Fallon's cellphone took that particular moment to jingle. She glanced at the number…the emergency desk. "Hello," she said.

"It's about to break loose down here," Emoline Putters said. "They've been trickling in, nothing we couldn't manage, but one of the beams in the lodge came down, and we have four firefighters injured, as well as three of the hotel personnel. Don't know the extent of the injuries, but Eric is coming in with them. ETA ten minutes or less."

"I'm on my way." She clicked off, torn between hurrying to the ER and staying here a minute or two, trying to comfort the little boy who'd crawled all the way under his covers now. Not even his head was showing. "Look, Tyler," she said, "I know you didn't start that fire. It was an accident in the kitchen. The grease got too hot and when that happens it can cause a fire."

"Really?" he said, still covered.

"Really. No one meant it to happen, and we know you didn't start it."

"That's why he doesn't want me," he said.

"Who?"

"My first dad...Donnie."

"Because of a fire?"

He didn't say anything, but she saw the blanket bob up and down and took that for a yes.

"Did you start a fire at your house?"

"He said so, but I didn't do it."

"What kind of fire?"

"In his chair. He was sleeping and it just caught on fire."

"In Donnie's chair," she said, just to be sure.

The blankets bobbed up and down again.

"And Donnie said you started the fire in his chair?"

"Said it was my fault 'cause I didn't get it. I was supposed to get it when he went to sleep, and I forgot."

"What, Tyler? What were you suppose to get?"

"His cigarette," he said, snuffling. "I always had to get his cigarette."

Fallon drew in a furious breath, trying to keep her voice calm for Tyler's sake. "So he'd go to sleep while he was smoking and it was your job to take the lit cigarette from him when he did?"

"Uh-huh."

Fallon's phone rang before she could respond. She glanced at the number. It was Emoline Putters, getting impatient, she guessed. "Look, Tyler, we know the fire up at the lodge wasn't your fault. Nobody's blaming you." While she truly wanted to comfort Tyler over what Donnie had done to him, and tell him that it wasn't his fault, that Donnie shouldn't have done that, it wasn't her place. Like

Edith had said, everybody needed a mother sometimes, but she wasn't Tyler's mother, and she had to remember that. Had to remember that the mothering instinct she felt toward him was because he was her son's brother. *But Tyler was not hers.* He belonged to James, and this was something James would have to deal with. "Look, I'll be back in a while, Tyler, and maybe you can show me how to play that game."

He poked his head out from under the covers. "I'll beat you," he warned.

She smiled. "I'm sure you will."

On her way back to the ER, she thought about the many ways she'd like to throttle that Donnie character, and every which way seemed too kind. A man like that deserved…

"From the look on your face, I'd say you're about to tie someone up with surgical tape," James said. He was bandaging the hands of the cook who'd tried dousing the grease fire with water. Not a good move. The fire had leapt from the pan. Luckily, the cook had managed to jump back far enough that his injuries weren't serious.

She went to the sink to scrub her hands. "Surgical tape's too good. I want something that'll hurt more coming off."

"Not for me, I hope," he teased.

"For Donnie."

"Donnie? As in…?"

"The man who *isn't* Tyler's father! Tyler thinks he'll be accused of starting the fire at the lodge," she said, trying to keep her temper in check, even though she was so angry she was almost shaking.

"I don't understand."

"I mentioned that we had to take care of people from the fire and he said he didn't start it. Because of the way he reacted, I asked him if he'd ever started a fire at his house, and he said his dad accused him of it. It seems one of Tyler's *chores* was to pull a burning cigarette from Donnie's lips if Donnie dozed off. Apparently once Tyler didn't do it and Donnie's chair caught on fire."

"Damn," James muttered, as he rolled gauze over the fleshy part of the cook's palm.

"I hated to leave him but we've got several people coming in at the same time and..."

"I understand," James said, through gritted teeth.

"He's fine, James. For now, he's fine."

"Plucking lit cigarette butts from the lips of his step-father... A mother who allows that..." He looked up at the ceiling, clearly trying to grapple with his emotions. "Nothing about him is fine, Fallon. The kind of life he has to live with his mother... The thing is, I should be there to help him, right now when he's afraid he'll be accused of starting the fire. But I'm not there, like I wasn't there when *you* needed me."

She stiffened. "Don't turn this into something about me! I told you I understood, James. Tyler needed you then, and you had to be with him. *He* needed you, and I was fine. And I'm pretty sure Tyler understands why you're not there now," she said, even though she knew James was right. Tyler needed his father...his real father. Right now. "Once Eric gets back, maybe you can go to him."

Maybe turned out to be a fantasy when seven patients rolled through the door, one after the other. Not only had Eric come in with them, so had Neil. "Fallon," Eric called, from down the hall. "I'll need you in room three. Get me an oxygen set-up and an IV."

"Fallon," Neil yelled, from the other end of the hall, "get respiratory therapy in here, stat."

"Fallon, we need bandages down here in exam two,

and can you check the vitals on the patient in exam one… he claims he has high blood pressure, and I'm afraid the stress of all this might be too much for him." That from Gabby.

And so went the next two hours, with Fallon running from place to place, being all things to everyone. In a spare moment James watched her. Simply leaned against the hall wall for ten seconds and observed—his first time ever to see what she did so well—and it took only a moment to understand why everybody in the hospital praised her so highly. Fallon was amazing. Absolutely everybody here on every medical level depended on Fallon to do, well, pretty much everything. And she did, without ever missing a beat. She responded to the doctors, took time to comfort the patients, directed the volunteers and nursing staff. Yes, she was truly amazing. And if he hadn't fallen in love with her all those months ago, he'd have fallen head over heels in love tonight.

Damn, he wanted to make things right with her. He wasn't sure how, wasn't even sure what, but there had to be a way. But he had to make things right for Tyler, too. And that thought overwhelmed him. Fallon…Tyler… How was he going to do it? How was he going to be everything both of them needed?

"I think you're good to go see Tyler," she said as she rushed by him. "No more burns coming in, and word from the scene is that there are no more casualties. So I'd say now is as good a time as any to get out of here."

He reached out and caught her arm. Stopped her and, surprisingly, she didn't yank away from him, as he'd expected her to do. In fact, she looked grateful for the momentary break. "You need to slow down," he said.

"I will."

"Now. You look…exhausted."

"And I feel exhausted, but it's almost over. All the serious injuries have been treated, and as soon as we get the barrage of minor injures taken care of, I'm going to take a break."

"How about I go check on Tyler for a minute then come back and take over Triage for you while you go put your feet up for a while? It's showing on you, Fallon. It's been months since you've worked this hard physically, and I'm worried."

"I appreciate that. And you're right. I *am* out of shape."

"Then for once you'll listen to someone else?"

Stubborn was what Edith had called her. She wore that with some amount of pride but sometimes it did get in the way. "I'll listen. But just this once, and don't get used to it."

James chuckled. "You do have your red-headed ways, don't you? I think one of the first things I liked about you was that stubborn streak. At least, some of it."

"I prefer to think of it as independent, not stubborn."

He chuckled again. "Like I said…" This was the old Fallon, and it was so nice to have her back. Even if only for a moment. "Look, let me get out of your way, go see Tyler. Then I'll be right back. OK? You're not going to go back on your word, are you?"

"No. Unless someone needs me."

No one needs you like I do, he thought. Then he spun away before he said the words aloud. But Fallon reached out, grabbed hold of his hand, and pulled him back to her.

"I know it's not the way you want it to be between us, James. And I know this is hard on you. But someday you'll realize that what we're doing now is the way it has to be. And in the meantime…" She stood on tiptoe and brushed a light kiss on his cheek. "Thank you. Thank you for caring about me, thank you for helping me and, most of all thank you for letting me be part of Tyler's life. He's an amazing little boy. So go. If he's awake, tell him I'm anxious for my first lesson."

"Lesson?"

"Video game. He's going to teach me how to play."

"Are we talking about *my* Tyler? The little boy who breaks things? *That's* the Tyler who offered to teach you how to play?"

"One and the same. We had a talk earlier, have a little bet going that he'll beat me."

James blinked hard. "Amazing. I can't even get him to talk to me, and here he's offering to play games with you? How'd you do that, Fallon?" He was surprised and, admittedly, a little hurt at the same time. Tyler wanting to teach Fallon was a good thing, but it would have been nice if Tyler had made the same offer to him. Of course, Fallon was Fallon, and everybody responded to her that way. He had. So why should Tyler be the exception?

She tossed James a sassy wink. "I'll never tell." This time she was the one who spun away from him.

As it turned out, Tyler was sound asleep when James finally got back to his room. So he stayed but a moment, pulled the covers up over him, gave him a light kiss on the forehead then returned to Fallon. When he found her, she was carrying a stack of IV set-ups to the central supply area. He took them from her then she was off to take a break. Like a whirlwind, James thought. Damn, he loved that whirlwind.

"You OK?" James asked.

She was studying the choices of soft drinks in the vending machine, trying to decide between the orange and the strawberry. She'd been standing and staring blankly at them for the past several minutes, almost too numb to think. "I'm fine. Just ready to call it a night and go home. Everybody has been seen, we've transported a few people to Salt Lake City, most of the volunteers have left. So, after a sugar boost from one of these cans, I'm out of here."

"And your friend Edith?"

"Good. Giving me hell for being so stubborn. But good. I'm going to make arrangements to send her to her sister in Florida for a few weeks. Edith needs some warm weather and sunshine, I think. She asked me to come along and be her private duty nurse." An intriguing idea, and a tempting one. But she'd had to turn it down because, well... she wasn't sure. Somehow she just couldn't bring herself to leave White Elk. Funny thing was, just a few days ago she'd have probably jumped at the chance to get away for a while. Now she couldn't. "All expenses paid. Beachfront cottage. Amazing restaurants. A dream come true."

"And?"

"And I turned it down. Arranged for Jessica Walthers to go in my place. She's a retired nurse, widowed. I thought the warm weather would do her some good."

"It wouldn't do you any good?" James asked, the corners of his mouth turning up.

Fallon looked away. "I have a job now."

"But Gabby's not in a big hurry. Besides, most of what you're doing to get her hospital set up could probably be done from a warm, sunny beach in Florida."

"I don't fly any more. Edith is going to fly."

"Take a train and meet her there. I'll bet it would be a nice, relaxing ride across country."

"So how's Tyler?" she asked, turning back to the drinks machine, trying to change the subject, trying to ignore what James was hoping to get her to admit—that she was staying because of him, because of Tyler. "Last time I looked in on him he was busy playing his game. Doing really well with it, too. He taught me a couple of things, then turned around and beat me. And had the audacity to laugh at me."

"I've never seen him laugh."

"I'm sorry, James. I never…"

"Don't be sorry. It's good he's comfortable with you. God knows, he's not with me. But if it's not me, I'm glad it's you, Fallon. I trust you with my son."

His words were like a sharp knife through her heart. Words that were meant well and turned into bitter, deep pain. "I, um…I want to go home," she said. "Get some sleep." Get away from James. Get away from the reminders.

"Then I'll drive you. And if you don't want me there, I'll come back and sleep in one of the on-call rooms… won't even try and persuade you to let me stay."

"I can drive myself."

"You're exhausted."

That, she was. And this was an argument she wasn't going to win because she was in no condition to drive.

"How about this? I'll take you home, and when we get there you can decide what you want to do with me? Fair enough?"

"I'm not going to send you away. But…"

"But you're still not easy with the decision of having me stay there…not when Tyler's not there."

"Maybe a little. But he'll be there in a day or so. And I want him to be comfortable, to be settled. And with Christmas coming…"

He shushed her with a finger to her lips. "One day at a time, Fallon. And on this day I'm taking you home to sleep. When you wake up, we'll decide what happens from there. OK?"

She nodded her agreement. He was so easy to give in to. And that was the problem. She wanted to give in. With James, she always wanted to give in.

Fallon slept the whole way home and, to be honest, she didn't remember getting out of the car and walking into her house. Surely, the brisk winter wind or the falling snow would have woken her up, but her first recollection when she finally opened her eyes was of her sofa. She was under the patchwork quilt she kept on the back of it, all comfy and safe. She was still tired, and a little achy from over-exertion. Most of all, though, she was really wishing the morning light wasn't peeking in through the living-room curtains because she wasn't ready to start the day.

"I didn't look when I undressed you," James said.

He handed her a mug of coffee, but she refused it. Instead, she peeked under the covers to find, much to her relief, that she was still dressed. No snow boots, no socks, but otherwise decent.

"You thought I'd strip you naked?" he teased.

"I don't know what you'd do." Finally, she snatched the mug from him and took a sip.

"Actually, what I did was carry you in from the truck."

"No, you didn't," she said, forcing herself to sit up.

"Well, somebody did. And I'm the only one here." He stepped back then grinned at her. "You've put on a couple pounds, Fallon. And I've got the sore muscles to prove it."

"I have not," she argued, realizing he was just trying to get a rise out of her.

"If that's how you want to argue this thing, that's fine with me."

"You!" she said, tossing a throw pillow at him. 'You always did like to goad me into things."

"Or out of things…like your clothes, if I recall. But that didn't take much goading, did it? In fact, I remember a few times when you—"

She thrust out her hand to stop him. Just like that, the light moment between them was over and all the bad things were weighing her down again. "Not the past, James. I don't want to talk about the past."

"Was it that bad for you, Fallon? Because I thought you were happy…we were happy together."

They had been. She had been. But that had been a different life. One to which neither of them could ever return. And the way this conversation was turning into those memories—that was the reason she couldn't be around him. It was too painful.

Fallon cleared her throat. "Is…um…is Tyler going to be released today?"

The expression on James's face shifted almost instantly, going from warm and caring to reserved. "Eric wanted to run another set of tests this morning…a fasting blood sugar in case his mood swings are coming from an onset of diabetes, but he'll release Tyler after lunch if nothing shows up. Under the present circumstances, I don't think we should come back here to stay. You need more rest, and—"

"We can get along, James. You can bring Tyler back here, and the three of us can get along."

"The three of us, maybe, but what about the two of us?" James sighed deeply, audibly. "I don't know any more, Fallon. One minute you and I are doing fine, then the next…" He walked away from her, went to the kitchen door, and stopped, but didn't turn back around. "Tyler responds to you. That's a good thing and I'd like to see if you can draw out more in him than I've been able to. I think he might warm up to the maternal instinct in you, and you do have that toward Tyler. It's pretty obvious. But this animosity between you and me…"

She was afraid of that, afraid that denying her maternal instinct wasn't enough. But what could she do? She was a mother without her baby, and he was a little boy without a real mother. Those were situations she couldn't change, situations that were causing what James was seeing. But it was temporary. Once James and Tyler found another place to live… "Not animosity, James. I don't have *any* bad feelings toward you. And for what it's worth, I want you to stay. I just don't want you and me to live in the past because we can't get that back."

He finally turned around. "Then why do I feel like I never lost it, Fallon? Because I still have the same feelings for you. Still have the same reactions whenever we're together."

"You'll move on. Once your relationship is more settled with Tyler, you *will* move on."

"The way you have? Because I hope to God that doesn't happen to me. I loved what we had, what we were. And I don't want to lose it or, worse, pretend it never existed."

"It existed," she said, praying the tears wouldn't come. But she could feel them, stinging in the backs of her eyes. "It existed then it was gone." But not forgotten. Never, ever forgotten.

But now it was a shadow. One that broke her heart.

CHAPTER SIX

"BASICALLY, he's healthy. Couldn't find a thing wrong with him except his blood sugar was a little off. But that could be stress working on him. I'd like to test him again in six months, after his life has settled down, and see what we get then. In the meantime, just make sure he gets a healthy diet, and you'll be fine." Eric sat the chart down on the desk. "And maybe I should prescribe the same for you, James. Because you're looking really stressed out."

"I am. I'll admit it. I'm living with Fallon, still in love with her and pretty much facing her brick walls every time I turn around. And I have a son who barely speaks to me, who's destructive, who may get yanked away from me at any minute if, or when, his mother decides she wants him again. I'd say that's stress."

Eric shook his head. "Anything I can do, James. Just name it, and I'll try my best."

"Do you know a good local lawyer? My last lawyer... well, let's just say that he went off to seek his fame and fortune chasing ambulances, which leaves me high and dry. And I really do need to file for custody before Shelly does whatever it is Shelly intends to do next."

"Actually, I have a great attorney—Jason Greene. Say the word, and I'll make a call."

James didn't even hesitate. "Make the call. I'm ready

for the battle, and I hope that the way Shelly has abandoned Tyler with me three times in six months counts for something. This attorney, Jason Greene, has to be good enough to make it count for something, because I want Tyler all the way. Full, permanent custody, with limited visitation from his mother and none from the stepfather of his."

Eric patted him on the back. "Jason's good enough. I'll call him this morning, see if he can get you in right away. He has a chronic upset stomach, a symptom of his profession, and he's had a few spur-of-the-moment appointments with me, so now it's payback time."

"You know, the longer I stay in White Elk, the more I like it. I think the lifestyle could be addictive. The people here sure are."

"That's why we're expanding our medical facilities. Once people stay here for a while, they never leave. It's what happened to me. Neil convinced me to come, give it a try. Now I own a hospital, I have a wife, I've just bought a new house." Eric smiled the smile of a contented man. "What can I say? Life in White Elk is good. I hope that happens for you soon, too."

"So do I, for Tyler. I think I'd like to raise him here. Look, I've got to make rounds in the pediatric ward. If Jason Greene agrees to take me on as a client, tell him I'll free myself up to meet him at his earliest convenience."

Jason Greene's earliest convenience turned out to be late afternoon and it was amazing how much better James felt after the appointment was set. For the first time in days he allowed himself to feel a little hopeful that this situation could work out for the both of them…him and Tyler. Father and son. Father and son and…Fallon. No! He wouldn't allow himself to think that. Not when he was more than willing to meet her in the middle, but the closer he got to that middle, the more she backed away. Right now, it was up to Fallon. Her steps to make. Her choices. Yet, he hoped…dear God, he really hoped…

"Ready to go home?" he asked Tyler, just as the lunch tray was being carried from his room. James noticed that Tyler hadn't eaten a bite. He'd also been told that Tyler had refused breakfast.

Tyler shrugged.

"Dr. Ramsey said you're good to go."

Tyler's reaction was to clutch the video game control tight to his chest. "Don't want to," he said. Not the words James wanted to hear, but at least Tyler was finally speaking. "Why not?" he asked.

"'Cause Fallon doesn't have games."

"I thought you liked Fallon."

Tyler shrugged.

"I'm pretty sure she likes you, even though you broke her shelves." He was sure Tyler liked Fallon, so this resistance came as a surprise. "And she's fixed up a room for you."

He shrugged again.

"And I think she wants to make a snowman with you."

He shrugged once more, but this time something about the snowman had, apparently, sparked his interest. "A little one?" Tyler asked.

"Not too little. One at least as big as you are."

"Or as big as you?"

Finally, his son was responding. "Well, I suppose you could make a snowman as big as me, but it might fall over."

"Head's too big," Tyler said shyly. Then giggled.

"What?" That was the first time he'd heard Tyler

giggle, or even seen him smile. It was a surprise that gave him hope.

"Head's too big, that's why it'll fall over."

"How about you make one, and I'll make one and we'll see which one won't fall over."

"Can Fallon make one, too?"

"Of course she can. But maybe we should keep a little secret from her."

Tyler eyes widened. "What?" he asked, almost whispering it.

"Maybe if we don't tell her that a big head is the reason it'll fall over, then she'll make the biggest head and hers will fall over first."

Tyler giggled again, but didn't answer. James could see the mischief dancing in his eyes for a moment. It was a good sign. After all these months it was a very good sign. "Let's get out of here, OK?"

Surprisingly, Tyler latched right on to James's hand. To casual observers in the hospital hallway who didn't know any better, they looked like a perfectly normal father and son.

"I'm so glad," Fallon said, resisting the urge to throw her arms around James's neck. It was her natural reaction, but she had to stop doing that, and after her last hug she'd reaffirmed her resolve. Shored it up, braced it with steel, braced it with steel again for an extra layer. "And Jason Greene's really good." They were speaking in hushed tones so Tyler wouldn't overhear. "Tyler needs to be in your custody no matter what, and the sooner the better. It scares me to death when I think that Shelly might come back here and get him. Especially after what he told me about how Donnie used to make him take the lit cigarettes from his mouth. That's a horrible thing to do to a child and I don't know how any mother would tolerate that."

"A good mother wouldn't," James said. "But who ever said Shelly was a good mother?"

"Well, it's started, James. And that's good. Tyler really needs to feel safe and secure, and Jason will be amazing. He has five children of his own, loves kids. He won't let Shelly get away with anything." Her gaze went to Tyler, who was sitting by himself, staring out the window. "Maybe I could watch Tyler for you during your appointment? I'm finished working for the day, so it wouldn't be a problem." There she was, getting involved again. One layer of steel slipping away and she was doing nothing to stop it. If she had any sense, she'd run upstairs, hide behind her locked door, and not come out.

"Actually, I wanted to take him with me. I need to find more ways to be with him when I'm not working. But you could come along, I know he'd love that. And maybe we could have dinner at Catie's Overlook afterwards."

It was a nice offer, but too cozy. She simply wasn't ready for anything like that. "Sorry, but I have dinner plans," she dodged. Dinner for one, whatever she could grab from her fridge. "But you and Tyler go, and enjoy yourselves. Tell Catie to give Tyler a piece of her extra-special chocolate cake." She said that purposely loud so Tyler *would* hear.

Tyler twisted ever so slightly to look at Fallon, fighting hard not to show too much interest in that chocolate cake but losing the battle the way most little boys would at the mention of something so yummy.

She tossed a knowing smile at James. "You know which one I'm talking about…three layers, all kinds of chocolate frosting?" With her hands, she gestured something that was a good three times the size of any cake Catie offered, and Tyler's eyes widened to twice their size. "The one that comes with a huge scoop of vanilla ice cream."

That was more than any child could take. Tyler finally turned the whole way around to face James. "Can I have chocolate ice cream instead?"

"If you're very polite when you ask Catie, and say please and thank you."

"I want Fallon to come, too," Tyler said. "So she won't find out while we're gone."

Fallon sensed a little conspiracy going on between father and son. "What don't you want me to find out?" she asked.

"Our secret."

Fallon winked at James then immediately looked back at Tyler. "You have a secret?"

He nodded, and kept a very serious face.

"Will you tell me your secret?"

Tyler shook his head then looked to James for approval. James gave him the thumbs-up sign, and nodded. "If I tell, then it's not a secret," Tyler explained very seriously to Fallon.

"But is it about me?" she asked.

This time Tyler merely shrugged. But he was trying to fight back a smile. And, oh, how she wanted to see that smile.

"So, if it's about me, should I know what it is?"

Tyler rolled his eyes up to James for help with this answer. And James answered. "But if you know what it is, then it's no fun any more."

"So, it's a fun secret?" Her question was directed at Tyler, who nodded his head. "But is it fun for you, or for me?"

"Me," he admitted. "And...him." He nodded toward James.

"Then what you're telling me is that it's the two of you against me?"

Both James and Tyler nodded. And when Fallon saw that, her eyes nearly filled with tears. They were so much alike. Looked alike. Acted alike. Same mannerisms. Same mischievous sparkle in their eyes. "OK, if that's the way you're going to be, then I might just have to come with you and eat all of Catie's chocolate cake before you have a chance to order some."

"It's about the snowman's big head," Tyler blurted quickly. "It makes the snowman fall over. Now can I have the cake?"

Fallon turned away abruptly. "This is so good," she whispered to James. "He's an amazing little boy," she continued, swiping away a tear threatening to slip down her cheek.

"Is Fallon crying?" Tyler asked James.

"Looks like she is."

"Am not," she denied.

"I'm sorry," Tyler said, slipping his hand into her. "I didn't mean to make you cry."

One tear turned into a waterfall, and she excused herself from the room before Tyler felt any worse. Right now she was just so darned happy for no reason she could understand that her cry was going to take a good half-dozen tissues.

"Happy tears," James reassured Tyler. "Women do that."

"Women," Tyler said, mimicking James's tone of voice. "They just do that."

James had to clear his throat and refocus, because he was about to do that, too.

* * *

The appointment with Jason Greene was short. Fifteen minutes was all it took then James was back in the waiting room, where Fallon was busy watching Tyler play with a video game. She'd decided to come with them, but only because Tyler had braved the stairs, knocked on her door, and asked her. "He said it's promising." James put on his jacket. "But there's a lot of research to do first. He thinks, though, that if everything is as I think it is, it could go my way because Shelly is establishing a clear pattern of behavior." A heavy sigh escaped him. "He warned me that it could be a long, expensive fight if she doesn't want to surrender custody, because oftentimes parents like Shelly who don't want their children will put up the fight anyway, for appearances or financial gain."

"And?"

"Let the fight begin, if that's what happens. It's not about the money and Jason said he's going to make sure it's not about what Shelly wants since she's proving she *doesn't* want Tyler. I'm actually conservatively optimistic about this, Fallon. Jason said I shouldn't start celebrating yet, but I feel like celebrating, anyway."

"Small celebration," she said, smiling.

His looked over at Tyler, who was so engrossed in some kind of virtual reality he hadn't even noticed James standing there. "I see video games in my future."

"Then be prepared to take a beating because he's good. And I'm not just saying he's good for a five-year-old. He's good for anyone."

"With all the bad things that have gone on around him, he's really struggling to be a normal little boy, isn't he? The kids I see in my practice are just like him…fixed on the games, paying no attention to the adults. Creating their own little worlds."

"He needs to be normal, James. Needs it all the time, not just when he's with you."

"Well, no matter what else is going on with Tyler, Jason's going to file for emergency temporary custody first thing tomorrow morning. He thinks I'll have a pretty good chance of having it granted this time, and that having temporary custody gives me a much stronger position when we get to the hearing for full custody. Besides, it's a good safeguard for Tyler. If Shelly does come back, I won't have to give him to her. She'll actually have to hire a lawyer and go to court to get him back as long as the temporary custody is in force."

Tyler glanced up at the mention of his name, clearly torn between what was being said about him and staying involved in the race between to two cars on the game screen. His car was winning. "What's good for me?" he asked, then immediately switched his attention back to the game.

"Staying with me without going anywhere else for a while."

With those words spoken, Tyler crashed his car and the game was over. He held onto the game controler for a little while, and the frown on his face clearly indicated he was thinking about what James had said. Finally, when he'd processed it, satisfied he understood, he looked up. "Like back to my mom and my old dad?"

"In a way," James hedged. "You OK with that, Tyler?"

Tyler responded with his typical shrug then stood up. "Are we still going to live with Fallon?"

"For a while, if she doesn't mind."

He shrugged that one off too. Gave a wistful glance over his shoulder at the video game set-up then headed for the door. "It's going to be boring," he muttered. "She doesn't have games."

Fallon bit back a laugh at that comment, and if the expression on James's face could have screamed anything, it would have screamed, *God, help me!* He held out his hand for Tyler, though, and for the second time Tyler took hold.

Fallon, bringing up the rear as they walked to the parking lot, brushed away a tear once more.

The walk to Catie's Overlook was pleasant. White Elk looked like Christmas now. Old-fashioned streetlamps were decorated with pine boughs and red ribbons, merchants' windows were strung with lights. The Christmas-tree festival was under way, where each little shop owner purchased a well-grown live tree, set it in front of his or her shop and sponsored the decorating. In other words, anyone who wanted could pay to decorate one of these trees, and the proceeds would go to charity, which, this year, was the pediatric ward at the hospital. And, more specifically, a program in the planning stages at present that would help children with juvenile diabetes. It was a good deed in that the cause was worthy but also a good deed in giving White Elk an authentic Christmas charm. With a nice dusting of snow covering everything, it was a fairyland. Beautiful. And if Fallon had been in a Christmas mood this year, this would have made her feel even more in the mood.

But she wasn't. Christmas just didn't mean anything now, the way it had never meant much when she'd been a child. Back then her Christmases had been filled more with sadness than anything else, because she had always been the child who hadn't belonged, the one who'd been staying with a distant relative, the child who hadn't fitted in. Usually the gifts she'd got had been last minute or thoughtless. Sometimes she hadn't got a gift...nobody had thought to buy one for the little girl who hadn't really belonged there. And to be honest, she didn't remember ever spending Christmas with the same people. One year she'd be packed off to distant cousin Flora, the next she'd end up with Great-Aunt Henrietta. And so her Christmases went. No fond memories.

But not for Tyler, if she had anything to do with it. If his Christmas memories from the past were bad, this would be the year they would be good. This year, and every year after, she hoped. Because now Tyler was in White Elk with his dad. And Christmas was about the little boy whose face was pressed to the toy-store window, looking at the toy train set he saw there and the box of building blocks. Being just like every other little boy at this time of the year. Like her little boy would have been... "I was thinking about a Christmas tree," she said, before the sad thoughts had time to take hold. "Do you think we should get a little one?"

Tyler rolled his eyes, but didn't offer an opinion.

"Maybe, instead of having a tree at home, we could sponsor one of the charity trees and decorate that?"

Tyler shook his head this time, and actually looked up at James, as if asking him to intercede here.

James looked at Fallon, winked. "Maybe we don't need a tree. I haven't had one since I lived at home with my parents, and I don't miss it. Instead of a tree, maybe we could buy a potted plant and hang a few glass balls on it. That would look like Christmas, wouldn't it?"

"But I want a *real* Christmas tree," Tyler cried. "A great big one! With lots of lights."

Was that the kind of tree he'd had with his mother and Donnie, or was that another of his wishes? Maybe one that had never come true. Fallon wondered if Tyler had ever had nice Christmases, or had they been miserable, like the ones she'd had when she'd been young? "You might have to help me move furniture so we can get a big one in the house."

Tyler nodded eagerly. "And throw some of it away if there's not room for the tree."

Fallon laughed. Well, the child was enthusiastic about something. And the way his eyes sparkled…he was James. Easy to love. "I think we'll manage without throwing away my furniture," she said. "And, Tyler, we're going to have to buy new decorations. I've always had a little tree and I don't have enough to decorate a big tree. So, will you be in charge of picking out the decorations?"

He hesitated for a moment, didn't respond as eagerly as she'd expected. Then he reverted back to his usual behavior. He shrugged, and totally zoned out of all the Christmas decorations strung up everywhere as they continued their walk to Catie's. The reaction of a child who'd built up hopes before then had them destroyed.

It was a delicate balance and she and James were going to have to be careful because, now that she'd started Christmas for Tyler, she didn't want to ruin it for him, too.

Pulling her scarf up tighter around her face to fight off the chilly air whipping around her, Fallon dropped back and walked behind James and Tyler, and twice, when James glanced over his shoulder at her, she feigned fascination with something in a shop window. Maybe she shouldn't have gotten involved. Because she was becoming almost as excited about Christmas as Tyler had been for a little while, and that wasn't good. She was used to living without the hopes and promises now, and here she was, building a few around something she couldn't have. And she really did want a Christmas tree…a big one. With lots of lights.

"He went right to sleep," James said, dropping down onto the couch next to Fallon, keeping his proper distance from her, of course. "I sat with him about five minutes, thought he might ask some questions about why he was going to keep on living with me for a little while, or maybe talk about the Christmas tree, but he just turned over on his side and went to sleep. It was a big day for him. I think we actually wore him out."

"He's had a turbulent life so far. He copes by acting out or by not acting at all. Probably the only two reactions in his young repertoire. And as far as the Christmas tree goes, I have an idea he's learned not to count on anything. If you don't count on it, you don't end up being disappointed." She raised her mug of hot chocolate to her lips, but paused before she took a sip. "It's not a mistake, is it, giving him this big Christmas?"

He laughed. "Giving a child a big Christmas? I think it's absolutely the best thing we can do for him. Tyler needs something to look forward to in his life. I don't think he's ever really had that."

"You, too," she added. "You need something to look forward to."

"And what about you? What do you need, Fallon?"

"Nothing. I never had good Christmases when I was growing up, and I don't need them now."

"I'm not talking about Christmas, specifically. What do you need in life, Fallon? There was a time I thought I knew, but maybe I was wrong. I mean, we talked about having a large family. You wanted a big house for all those children we were going to have. You didn't want to quit work because you were totally devoted to the idea that a woman is capable of doing everything she wants. But now I don't know if that's what you need in your life, and I want to know. It bothers me that I don't. Or that I might have been wrong all along."

She bristled. "This isn't about me. I invited you to live here because it was supposed to be about Tyler. *Only Tyler.* And I don't want you to make this about something it's not."

He held up his hand to stop her. "Whoa, there. You really do have a way about turning a nice, innocent conversation into something adversarial, don't you?"

"It wasn't innocent, James. When you made it about me, it was anything *but* innocent. You know you were trying to manipulate me, trying to take advantage of the moment to pry into something that's none of your business any more."

"What if that's what I was doing? I'm not admitting it, but for the sake of the argument, what if I did try to make it about you? Is that really so bad?"

"It is when I laid down the ground rules about you staying here."

"Fallon! For God's sake. We've made love. I've seen that little heart-shaped birthmark on your back. Doesn't that give me some rights?"

"No," she snapped. "That was then. This is…this is another time, another life. And you know my terms, James. If you can't live with them, I won't kick you out, but I'll take a room at the lodge until you and Tyler can make better arrangements."

"But aren't you the one who keeps stepping over the line? Be honest with yourself, Fallon. Aren't you the one who keeps getting involved?"

"With Tyler. I'm getting involved with Tyler."

"But getting involved with Tyler is getting involved with me."

That much was true. And she'd have to try harder to stop it. "I think I can separate the two of you."

"I don't believe that! Sometimes when I see the way you look at him, there's such longing. And I remember that look, Fallon. Used to see it when we talked about our future. Talked about the children we wanted to have and the life we wanted to build for them."

"You're wrong, but go ahead and believe whatever you want. I really don't care!"

James ran a frustrated hand through his hair. "OK, that little heart on your back aside, we had something good going on between us. I messed up after your accident, but I thought we could put that behind us and move on from there. Hoped we could, anyway."

"We can. I'm *not* angry that you had to choose Tyler over me. That's what you should have done...what you should always do. But, James, that was so long ago, and I've been through so much. I can't be *that* Fallon any more. She's gone. She's not coming back."

"She's not that far away, Fallon," he said gently. "I see her all the time, when she's not trying to be so... guarded."

Unfortunately, that was the problem. She couldn't hide from James. Couldn't hide anything. "Not guarded, James. Just not the same. And that's what you've got to understand. So back to your original question... What do I want? I want the best Christmas ever for Tyler. I want him to be with someone who cares enough to help him build some hopes."

"The way you do?" he asked gently.

"The way *you* do," she replied.

"Like a real family," James said. "A real family for Christmas."

"For Tyler," she reminded him "Like a real family *for Tyler*, for Christmas." To think of it in any other way hurt too much.

"Then tell me what happens when Tyler starts loving the mother in this little Christmas family, and she eventually walks away from him?"

"Are you talking about you, or Tyler?" she asked, pushing herself off the couch. "Because if we want to help Tyler, we've got to get over this. *You've* got to get over it." *She* had to get over it.

"As in getting over *you*? Is that what you mean?"

"Something like that."

He shook his head. "You know what, Fallon? Your friends have given you a lot of slack because of the accident. They've done everything you wanted them to do because they loved you, even if what you wanted essentially pushed them away, maybe even hurt them. I don't know why you keep pushing people away, and I don't want to argue about it. But I'm not giving you that same slack. You can't tell me to get over you and expect that I'll just do it because you want me to. It doesn't work that way. Not when I love you. And I do love you. So, no, I'm not getting over you. Like I've said, already, and I'll keep saying, I'll respect the distance you want…the boundaries you've built up around yourself. But you can't tell me how I have to feel about you. You don't have that right." He stood, too. "Look, I'm going for a walk, to clear my head. I'll be back in half an hour." Then he threw on his jacket and walked out the front door. More like strode out the front door, with every harsh footstep she heard on the hardwood floor a testament to exactly what he was feeling.

In a small way she was flattered. In an even bigger way she was scared. Not because he'd told her off. But because he'd been right. About everything. Except him being right about everything still didn't make things right in her life. Because nothing there was right, and she still didn't believe it could be right ever again. Not without James…and Tyler. Not without James Allen Galbraith, Junior. But that's the way it was, whether or not James Allen Galbraith, Senior, liked it or not.

Three hours of tossing and turning, and she was barely asleep when the first crash startled her awake. The second one sent her over the edge of the bed and scurrying to pull on her bathrobe. The third crash propelled her out her bedroom door and straight to the top of the stairs, where she looked down and saw James, dressed in boxer shorts and a T-shirt running for the kitchen. He didn't look like he'd had much sleep either.

Fallon padded down the stairs, wondering if her bare feet would be safe, considering what she expected to find in the wake of Tyler's tirade, and fell into step behind James who, she had to admit, looked downright sexy first thing in the morning. Sexy and, right this moment, ready to explode.

"Tyler," he called on his way through the kitchen door. "What are you doing?"

Fallon, who was so close behind him she could practically smell his aftershave, bumped right into the back of him when he stopped dead in his tracks. She braved a peek around James, expecting the worst, only to see Tyler standing there amid a clutter of pots and pans all over the floor, along with spilled silverware and practically every utensil she'd had in the drawer. But on the counter were three bowls, filled to the top with breakfast cereal and overflowing with milk, which was dripping down into the open, and empty, utensil drawer. Along with the cereal were three slices of bread smeared from crust to crust with strawberry jam…jam that was likewise slathered across a good portion of the counter top. And there were three poured glasses of orange juice, with a fair measure of juice trickling down the front of the cabinet.

It was a spectacular mess to behold, and Tyler was standing in the middle of that mess, grinning from ear to ear—his first real grin. He'd fixed them breakfast.

"It looks delicious," she said quite brightly as she stepped away from James and pulled a kitchen stool over to the breakfast counter. As delicious as any breakfast could look at three in the morning, given the disheveled condition of her kitchen.

James chuckled. "Looks like the best breakfast I've ever had at this time of the day." He followed Fallon's cue and pulled up a kitchen stool for himself then one for Tyler. And the three of them sat down together and ate breakfast in the middle of a mess that was going to require about an hour's worth of cleaning and showers for everybody. "So, why'd you do such a nice thing for us?" James asked, choosing careful words as he picked up the piece of bread that nearly collapsed under the weight of the jam on it.

"Wanted to," Tyler replied.

"And I, for one, am glad to have another cook in the house," Fallon chimed in. Where she was sitting, a little stream of juice once flowing in one direction had redirected itself and was fast closing in on her. Rather than cleaning it, she scooted over, which brushed her right into James. Either he didn't notice or he was the best impostor in the world, because he simply plopped his piece of jammed-up bread into his mouth and didn't so much as flinch over the fact that Fallon was nearly draped over his lap.

"Can we go find a Christmas tree after breakfast?" Tyler asked shyly.

James and Fallon looked at each other then smiled. "Can we take a little nap first?" Fallon asked. "Get rested up so we can have lots of energy to find the biggest one?"

Naturally, Tyler looked disappointed. He'd had a plan, but now it was being put off. In his mind, having it put off was the same as not having it happen at all, and Fallon couldn't stand that. "As soon as it's light. There's a Christmas-tree farm about twenty miles from here, and we can go pick out the perfect one as soon as we can see everything they have. OK, Tyler? They won't let us pick out a tree if it's not light out, so it'll be up to you to come tell us when it's light. Can you do that?" The child *needed* to know that what he wanted mattered.

Tyler shrugged. But James didn't let him get away with being noncommittal.

"It's up to you, Tyler. OK, or not?"

"OK," he said tentatively.

"Well then," Fallon said, standing, ready to go back upstairs and leave the mess to James, who already sensed it would be his job to clean it up, "I'm going to go back to bed, and dream about Christmas trees. And I'm leaving the scrubbing of the kitchen up to you two." With that, she walked over to Tyler and gave him a kiss on the forehead.

"Him, too," Tyler said. "He needs a kiss, too."

"Yes, I do," James prodded. "I need a kiss, too."

"Right here," Tyler said, pointing to the spot on his forehead she'd kissed him.

James mimicked that. "Right here, and remember, it's about Tyler."

She sighed heavily, narrowed her eyes in protest as she approached James. Then aimed for his forehead, but got intercepted when he tilted his head back enough that her kiss caught him on the lips. And lingered a while. Long enough that she relaxed into the kiss, and James relaxed into the kiss, and they both totally forgot about Tyler for a moment. Then…

"Can I go move the furniture to make room for the tree?"

Both James and Fallon turned their heads toward the little boy at the same time, and answered in unison, "No!" Ten seconds later, Fallon was on her way back to her bedroom, her face flushed, her breaths short, her pulse racing. She needed a door. A big, heavy door to shut and lock. One for her heart, too. And a good place to throw away the key.

CHAPTER SEVEN

"It's a huge decision," Fallon said, smiling. They'd been looking at trees for almost an hour, after being the first ones lined up to get into the Christmas-tree farm. Now, after searching row after row of greenery that all looked pretty much the same to her, give or take a few scrawny exceptions, Tyler was still in decision mode, taking his job seriously. In fact, he was very methodical in the way he went about scrutinizing the various trees and tying scraps of fabric on the ones he was keeping under consideration. James was busy marking their location on a map provided by the owners of the tree farm.

"And I'm going to be late for work if he doesn't hurry up," James said, as he plotted the tenth tree.

"You've still got an hour before you have to go, and according to Tyler's calculation that's at least a dozen more trees." She grinned. "But isn't this fun?" Actually, it was. She'd never seen so many Christmas trees, didn't know that places like this existed. Her tree was stored in a small box in her attic. Fresh trees, with the luscious pine scent, were practically a novel concept for her, and she was in love with the idea of having a fresh tree in her home.

"And this farm has a good five hundred more acres of trees which, by *my* calculations, will take us about three more days to look at." He grinned back. "Think they'll let us camp here tonight?"

Fallon laughed. "If you think this is taking a long time, wait until we go to the Christmas store in town and he gets to pick out the ornaments. I predict at least two days there, and I'm pretty sure *they* won't allow camping."

James moaned then plotted yet another tree Tyler had tied a piece of white cloth on. "Seriously, we've got to bring an end to this if I'm going to have to chop it down then get it tied to the car and hauled back to your house."

"And remove all the markers on all the trees Tyler tagged."

James moaned once more. "Why do I have the feeling this is getting out of control?"

"That's what raising a child is about," she said. "Everything getting out of control. However, you're supposed to look like you're in control even when you're not, and when you're not you're supposed to act like you are so the child won't find out. Because if he does figure it out, he'll take control of you *and* the situation. So it's all about perceptions. If the child perceives you to be in control, even if you aren't, you're fine."

"And that flawed logic is exactly the reason I wanted to have ten or twelve children with you. You're such a good advocate."

Even though he'd meant nothing by those words, they did sting, and reflexively Fallon stepped away from James. She didn't mean to be so sensitive, didn't want to spend the rest of her life overreacting to perfectly innocent words, but she couldn't escape her reaction. It simply happened.

"Damn," he muttered. "I didn't mean to say that."

"It's fine," she said, stepping even farther away from him. One slow step at a time, with only her footprints in the snow to remind her how close she and James had been standing to each other. "Look, I have another suggestion. They'll dig the tree out for us and deliver it. We can put it in the house, keep it alive then plant it somewhere later. A tree Tyler will be able to keep as a reminder of his first Christmas with you."

"I'm sorry, Fallon. I really didn't mean to—"

She thrust out her hand to stop him. "I *said* I'm fine. Let's just leave it at that. OK?"

"But we'd talked about having children, Fallon. I remember telling you what a great mother you'd make. It was that day—"

"I remember the day," she snapped. Remembered it vividly. On a hike in the mountains, they'd run into a dozen little boy scouts. Cute, vivacious, having the time of their lives looking for a good campsite to spend the night. She and James had fallen in with the boys, hiked a couple of miles with them and she hadn't been sure she was going to be able to pull James away when it came time to part, he'd been having so much fun. That's the first time she'd thought she might wants lots and lots of children with him. They hadn't been engaged to be married, and most people would have said they were too new in their relationship to be thinking about children. But she was thinking about it anyway. And again, later, when James had mentioned wanting their very own little scout troop. He'd proposed a dozen children, which hadn't been serious. But she'd watched him in his element, seen his true heart with those children. So they'd talked a little that night. Tossed out funny names like Mortimer, Aloysius and Shadrach. Then settled on James, Junior.

Perfect thoughts for perfect days. And now those thoughts were all sad. "We talked about a lot of things, but that was a long time ago. And we were different people then."

"No," he said gently, "we *weren't* different people.
You may think we were, *or you were*, but those same two
people are standing right here, being awkward with each
other for no reason. And I'd built some hopes and dreams
around *us*. Counted on us being together. The only difference between me then and now is that back then I had
something I wanted so badly I ached for it, and I thought I
was going to get it. I still ache for it Fallon, but the change
in me is that I don't know if I will get it. You tell me I
won't, but I'm not ready to believe it yet."

"Believe it, James." She glanced out at Tyler, who
seemed to have settled on *the tree*. At least, the jumping up and down and excitement he was showing over a
particularly bushy one seemed to indicate he had. Long
needles, a beautiful bluish-green, and with some artful
trimming just about the right size, it seemed to be a perfect
tree. "Counting on too much can get you hurt," she said.

"Or it can lead to everything you've ever wanted. I'm
not ready to give up."

"I'm sorry it's turned out the way it has." Sorry for
James, sorry for herself.

"It hasn't turned out any way yet, Fallon."

He stepped up to her, and ran his thumb down her
cheek, a gentle stroke she remembered and loved. "Don't,"
she whispered. "We shouldn't have yesterday, and we
can't...not again."

"Don't what?" he asked, tracing his thumb along the
contour of her jaw then moving his touch ever so slightly
underneath. "Don't do this?" He tilted her head up and
kissed her on the lips. Tiny butterfly kisses that caused her
to shiver. "Is that what you don't want me to do because
you always enjoyed that, didn't you?"

Fallon willed herself to speak, willed herself to break
free of his spell, but she couldn't.

"Or is this what you don't want?" He pressed his lips harder to hers this time. Parted her lips with his tongue and met her tongue in an instant fury.

Her hands snaked around his neck and her fingers inched upwards, entwining in his hair, massaging his scalp. Bodies pressed tighter, and even through the bulk of their jackets she could feel his erection pressing against her pelvis. She pushed into him, deepened the kiss, groaned.

But then he pulled back. "Is that what you don't want, Fallon? Because from this side of the kiss, I felt you kissing me back."

She wanted to be the one who took a step back now, but there was nothing in her that forced her to move. She could barely breathe. Barely focus. Barely think. Because James was right. She was kissing him back. And more. Just like always, this was where it had started with them. A simple kiss was never simple. A fond embrace was always filled with the expectation of so much more. "What I used to enjoy has nothing to do with the way things are now," she finally managed to choke out.

"Used to enjoy, Fallon? There were two people in that kiss, and both of them were enjoying it. So, the way things are now is that you're resisting me. For whatever reason, and I wish to God you'd be honest with me about it, you're resisting me."

She braced herself to the next part of the round. "And what would you have had me do when you kissed me? Slap you in front of your son? He's looking at us right now, you know that, don't you? Do you really want me to put on a spectacle for him, because I can do it."

James stepped back, blew out an exasperated breath. "Why has it become such a battle between us? I love you, I'm pretty sure you still love me. So shouldn't we be able to find something in there that's simple? A place where we can start from that and rebuild what we had, or what we were trying to have, before your accident?"

"Nothing's ever simple, James. If there's one thing I learned when I was a child, that's it. Nothing is ever simple, and there's no point in pretending that it can be." She pulled up her scarf. "I think Tyler has found his tree, so I'm going to go make arrangements to have it delivered."

James didn't respond, but the look on his face, as he turned to go after Tyler said it all. She'd slapped him without raising her hand. Maybe that was a good thing. Maybe now he'd leave her alone. Or alone long enough to get her armor up again. This time, though, she'd have to put on the whole armor rather than the bits and pieces she'd donned before in the hope that was enough. Because it was clear it wasn't enough. Which meant she now had to gird herself to go the distance because if she didn't, she'd end up hurting the person she loved most in the world. Her armor...it was to protect James. Not her. She'd faced the facts...*her facts*...months ago. They might be living as a family now, but it was only for show because Tyler needed the solidarity for a time. As soon as James was able to find a place for the two of them, she'd put an end to it once, and for ever.

That's the only way it could be because of what she'd done. This was for James. Only for James.

Eight hours into his shift and he was restless. He wanted to go home. "Home," he muttered, on his way down to exam three to treat a two-year-old with sniffles. "Like I've got a home."

"You need a place to stay?" Emoline Putters asked, as he passed by her desk. "Because I've got a big old house up on Ridgeview Road just sitting empty. Too big for me now that my husband is gone, and I hated rattling around in there all by myself, so I took an apartment closer to the hospital, and haven't gotten around to doing anything with the house. But it's got all my furniture, and it's in good shape, if you want to rent it. Or even buy it."

It wasn't what he wanted to hear, because he didn't want to move out of Fallon's cabin. It was too small for the three of them, though. And the tension building up...

"Big yard, too, for that boy of yours. Part of it's fenced in. Did that when my own children were young. The back of the property backs up to several acres of woods leading up into the foothills a piece. Nice place for a boy to go tromping around with his dad. Had a lot of good years in that house, and now it's time to let another family enjoy it."

Another family...his family of two. "Sounds perfect, Emoline. I'd like to take a look. Might take me a couple days to find a hole in my schedule, though. We're getting into the cold and flu season, and the clinic's pretty backed up right now." One step. That's all it was. He was going to look at a house. One step, but it was a big one.

"Sure. Stop by my desk later, and I'll give you the keys. You can go take a look when you're ready."

"How long has it been empty?"

Emoline Putters, usually prickly and irascible, drew in a deep breath, and at the end of it there was sadness on her face. A sadness that told James so much about her. She'd loved deeply, and hadn't gotten over the loss of that love. "Going on to five years now. Ed Lester, the head of hospital maintenance, goes up every couple of weeks and looks after it for me because I haven't been able to do anything about it. But I think you'd be good there, and it's time for that old house to see some new life."

Impulsively, James gave the woman a hug and, surprisingly, she didn't stiffen under his embrace, as he'd expected from her. It occurred to him that she wasn't prickly and irascible as much as she was lonely, and trying to hide it. She'd mellowed, though. Found the right time, and the right reason, and mellowed, the way he hoped Fallon would. "I appreciate the offer," he said. "And I'll get up there as soon as I can."

"Where you need to get is down to exam three. They've been waiting too long for you, and there's no excuse to keep a sick child waiting all this time."

She cleared her throat, thrust the patient chart at him and marched away, all prickly again. Except James knew better about Emoline. Just the way he knew better about Fallon. It did make him wonder, though, why Fallon was set on imitating Emoline Putters...being all prickly and irascible. Emoline, as it turned out, had a side to her he hadn't known. So was there a side to Fallon he'd never seen? Something he didn't know, or she didn't want him to know?

"We'll go just as soon as I make one more phone call," Fallon promised. Tyler had been having a fit all morning. He wanted to bring the tree inside, he wanted to move the furniture. He really wanted to go buy decorations, and he'd been very loud about that. Loud about being bored. Loud about not having a video game to play with. Loud... And she was getting a headache, because everything she'd planned for her day had gone bust. Each and every time she'd picked up the phone, he'd knocked something off the shelf. When she'd picked up her catalogs to peruse the pages for various obstetric exam tables, he'd started stomping around the house so loudly she hadn't been able to concentrate. Hours of this, and she was at her wit's end.

She understood that he was bored. She honestly did feel badly about that because there was nothing here for a five-year-old to do. No toys, no children to play with. No nothing! And to top it off, she couldn't even allow him to go outside and play in the snow because her yard wasn't fenced and she didn't have time to watch him. As little as he'd slept last night, and as early as he'd gotten up this morning, she'd thought he'd be ready for a nice, long nap. But when she'd suggested it, he'd put his hands over his ears then started yelling.

The final straw was a preliminary interview for the post of chief of nursing. She was trying to prequalify a candidate by phone, so the woman wouldn't have to make the long trip there before Fallon was able to check her credentials and get recommendations. In the middle of the ten-minute interview Tyler had unplugged the phone. Actually, not unplugged it so much as ripped it from the wall. So now she needed a service call to repair the damage, and she was reduced to using her cellphone, which had marginal reception out here.

"I don't want to wait," Tyler said sullenly. "You promised to take me, and I want to go now!"

"I know I promised, but—"

"Nobody ever does what they say," he grumbled.

That caught her attention. And she wondered if Tyler might be reacting from some of the tension between her and James. It was certainly a possibility. He'd built up a few hopes, and with the way she and James were getting along now saw the possibility that he'd be let down yet again. "Who never does what they say?"

"Everybody. They promise me I can stay this time then I can't. And they promise me they'll quit yelling, but they never do."

His home. He was talking about his home…his other

home with his mother. So much insight in so few words. And now she felt terrible, because she knew, for certain, that Tyler was feeling that same kind of insecurity here. While she and James had been saying this was about Tyler, they'd turned it into something about them and Tyler was watching from the sidelines. "Well, I don't break my promises, Tyler. Occasionally it takes me a while to get to them, but I always do. Here's the thing. Sometimes I'm not sure what a boy your age needs to be doing. I never had any little brothers, don't have any little boys of my own…so once in a while someone has to tell me. But not by yelling, and stomping around the house."

"How?" he asked.

"By telling me. Just say, *Fallon, I need something to do.*"

He thought about it for a moment and she could see the concentration in his eyes as he analyzed all sides of what she'd just told him. He was so much like James. The more she got to know Tyler, the more she saw the similarities.

"Fallon, I need something to do," Tyler finally said. He didn't sound sure of himself. It was like he was trying out the concept to see if it worked, to see if she kept her word.

"Tyler, I just happen to have something for you to do."

His eyes lit up. "You do?"

"I think you need to go sledding. And, as luck would have it, I have an old sled in the storage shed out back."

"What's that?" he asked, still cautious.

"You've never heard of a sled?"

He shook his head.

"It's better than a video game. Actually, it's almost like a video game, only instead of you pushing the buttons that make the game do different things, you're the one who's doing everything."

The look on Tyler's face showed marginal interest, mixed with healthy skepticism.

"Want me to prove it to you?"

He shrugged. Still didn't believe she was about to make good on her promise. Poor child. He was too use to being let down and it just made her ache for him. "It's up to you, Tyler. If you want something to do, this is all I've got right now."

"I'll go sledding," he said, much too reserved for a five-year-old on the verge of an adventure.

"Good choice." Fallon reached out to pat him on the back, but he jerked away. "So, do you have any boots?"

He shook his head.

"Mittens, scarf, hat?"

No again.

"Then I'd say we run to town and buy you some sledding clothes. Is that OK with you?"

Twenty minutes later they were barely inside the mercantile when Dinah Ramsey and her twin daughters Paige and Pippa practically pounced on them. Dinah immediately ran to Fallon and pulled her into her arms. "Are you OK?" she whispered. "You look like you've seen a ghost."

"Tension. It's not so good between James and me, and I'm worried about Tyler. I think what James and I are going through is affecting him."

"And he reminds you of your own little boy?"

"My own little boy never drew a breath!" she said, stiffening.

"Your child is your child, Fallon. You and James should have grieved together."

Fallon turned her head, blinked back the tears.

"Sometimes when I watch Tyler I think that he could have been mine. And it hurts so bad."

"But isn't this something you and James should be going through together?"

"What I did to him…"

"Fallon, you were fighting for your own life from all the injuries. And fighting to keep your baby at the same time. You were confused, and no one could blame you for your decisions. I mean, I can't even begin to imagine what you experienced, what you were thinking. And I'm sure if James knew…"

"That's the thing. He should have known. It wouldn't have made a difference in the way things turned out, but he had a son he didn't know about. And I've seen how hurt he was by what Shelly did to him. So how could I put him through that again, especially when *our* son didn't survive?"

"I think you're underestimating him."

"I think I'm protecting him."

"But does James really need protection, Fallon? Think about it."

"That's practically *all* I think about, and I'm…"

"Scared to death?" Dinah asked. "Afraid that if you tell James he had a son who died, James will quit loving you?"

"I don't know, Dinah. I really don't know."

"Well, the one thing I know is that our children are getting impatient." They glanced at the trio, Tyler, Pippa and Paige, who were glaring back at them.

"I promised Tyler we'd go sledding, and he's used to having promises broken."

"Well, I have a fantastic idea. I'm going to take the girls sledding out on Porter's Bluff. It's a mild little hill, perfect for younger children. How about I take Tyler with us? He

seems to be getting along well with them and maybe…"
Dinah hesitated.

"It will do him good to get away from me?"

"Maybe it will give you and James some time to talk.
Alone."

It made sense, but the only thing was, she was scared to
death of time alone with James. Of course, she could shut
her office door and work. That, if nothing else, was the
incentive she needed to let Dinah take Tyler for a while.
"He throws tantrums," she warned.

"Eric's told me."

"And breaks things."

Dinah nodded, then laughed. "And the twins will out-
number him two to one. I think we'll manage."

"Let me ask him, then." She watched Tyler and the girls
for a moment, and saw a little boy who was just like any
other little boy his age should be. Boasting to the girls,
showing off for them, happy, carefree. Tyler desperately
needed a normal life, one he could count on. So did she.

"Tyler," she said, bending down next to him, "would you
like to go sledding with Paige and Pippa? Mrs. Ramsey
has offered to take you with them, but I wanted to ask you,
as I'd promised to take you, too."

He glanced at the girls then back at Fallon. "I'll go with
them. They have three different kinds of sleds, including a
round one, which they say goes faster than a regular one,
and all you have is a regular one."

From the child who'd never heard of sledding to the
one who was a five-year-old expert. The transformation
was amazing, and Fallon was pleased with her decision.

She was still smiling about it two hours later when
James wandered in, surprised not to find Tyler there. "Two
very pretty young girls had their sway. He chose them over
me, and Dinah called a few minutes ago to say that they're

all going out for pizza later, so it looks like the old folks are left home, alone for the evening."

"What you're telling me is that he's on a date with twins? Isn't that every grown man's fantasy?"

"He's quite the ladies' man. I mean, he perked right up for them, put on his best manners, puffed out his chest, did some bragging. You know, the typical thing all men do when they're around pretty girls."

"Well, how about I put on my best manners, puff out my chest, and take you up to Pine Ridge for dinner? Not a date. Just two people in need of a meal."

It was tempting. It had been so long since she'd had a real night out...probably her last night out with James all those months ago. Admittedly, getting out more these past days was feeling so good. But this?

"We could sit at separate tables," he said, grinning. "Me at one, you at the one behind it with your back to me."

"I'm not *that* bad," she said, laughing.

"You're doing a lot for me, Fallon, and taking you to dinner is the least I can do to show you how much I appreciate everything."

"We do need to talk about some things, because I think Tyler is picking up on our tension. Maybe we can figure out how to make it better for him." She turned to the picture window, her back purposely to him. When she faced him, when she looked into his eyes, she couldn't resist. And she had to keep her head about this.

"I wish you wouldn't turn away from me, Fallon."

He stepped up so close behind her she could feel the sparky little prickles on her flesh he always caused when he was so close. She remembered that feeling, savored it. *Wanted it.* But being alone with James was too difficult and, as much as she didn't want to go out with him, she didn't want to stay in with him even more. "Let me call Angela," she said in response.

"Angela?"

"Angela Blanchard. She's the executive chef. There's a certain table…"

James stepped back. "I know. In the corner, facing a wall, behind a potted palm. Something that would never be construed as romantic."

She spun to face him, saw a rare flash of anger cross his face. As much as she hated seeing it, she was glad. Perhaps, at least, James was beginning to realize that there was no relationship between them other than friendship. "Actually, that would be a nice table, except I don't think they have one in that spot. I was going to ask for the one near the fireplace, away from the window. I'm still not ready to face that view yet. It overlooks the Middle Sister where…" Where everything about her life had changed.

The hard lines on his face softened. "I didn't know. Would you rather we simply stay in?"

Staying in came with more peril than going out. Either way, she'd have to cope with something she didn't want to. Staying here with James and risking the overtones of that, or facing a view of the thing she wasn't sure she could ever look at again?

Why was it that lately her life had been reduced to choosing between the lesser of two things she didn't want? For her, one choice held the promise of mortal terror, while the other choice promised an agony like nothing she'd felt throughout her entire ordeal. Either way, she couldn't win. But neither could James, and that's what bothered her most.

CHAPTER EIGHT

FALLON chose dinner at the restaurant. James figured that for her the choice was the lesser all of her perceived evils. And now, thirty minutes later, they were seated at a comfortable table for two in front of the massive stone fireplace in what was unquestionably White Elk's most romantic restaurant. The music playing in the background was a soft, sexy jazz, the chef's special *du soir* was a Chateaubriand for two, and the compliments of the chef was a bottle of champagne. If there could have been anything else spelling out a cozy, romantic evening, he wasn't sure what it was. Until…a bouquet of roses arrived at the table. From Angela, not from him. But the look on Fallon's face when they arrived was so close to panic that he almost wished he hadn't suggested this. *Almost*. Because, honestly, it was nice being out with her this way. And he hoped that somewhere during the evening she would loosen up and enjoy herself. Fallon was so tight, so full of stress and, if anything, as the days rolled by, it seemed to be getting worse.

"Are you nervous with me right now?" James asked. He knew she was. Anyone looking at her could see it—the way she clasped her hands so tightly, the way she frowned. But she'd have been nervous spending the evening alone with him in the cabin, too. Or nervous if they'd gone to have pizza. Or if she'd spent her evening locked in her office and he'd spent his shut behind the door in the den. Truth was, any close proximity to him, whether it was across the table, the next room, or the next block over, and she would be nervous. He did that to her now. He hated it that he did that. Wanted to change it. But so far he was failing miserably.

"No. Well…maybe, a little."

Her head was tilted down and he desperately wanted her to hold her head high, to look at him eye to eye the way she used to. But she was afraid to, and he'd seen that fear in her. That's what he didn't understand, couldn't figure out. They had differences, that much was painfully obvious. But this fear he kept sensing? What did she think she had to fear from him? It put him on edge. Made him nervous because he had to choose careful words, had to look at her carefully, had to adopt careful gestures. And he was also nervous for fear he'd slip. It was an onerous task and he hated always having to be on his guard with her. Hurting Fallon in any way, though…he wouldn't do it. Which meant that if he wanted her company, he'd have to continue being careful. "It's just dinner, Fallon. Two people eating together. No pressure from me, I promise."

"It's a *candlelit* dinner, James. With champagne. And have you listened to the music in the background? If that's not meant to seduce some man's lady love into bed this evening, I don't know what is."

"I'm not trying to seduce you, if that what you think I'm doing."

"Aren't you?" she asked pointedly.

"If you could see the way you look right now, with your arms folded across your chest, your shoulders so rigid, sitting on the edge of the chair, looking like you're ready to run at the first little provocation…believe me, even the most insensitive of men would pick up *those* clues. And I have picked them up, so you don't have to worry. I'm only here to eat."

"If I make your evening so miserable, why do you want to spend it with me?"

"Because I'm hoping that at some point during the evening you'll relax. We used to have a good time together, even when the intention was not to run home and make love. And I want that again for us. Even if we can't be one of the romantic couples, I'd like to be one of the friendly couples. Or at least make people believe you can tolerate my company for a few hours."

"You know I can tolerate your company, James," she whispered.

"Sometimes I don't know that any more," he said, wishing they could move on past this. That wasn't going to happen, though. Not tonight. No time in the foreseeable future either. "I mean, I know what we had at first happened like a tornado—fast, with so much passion. In retrospect, maybe it was too intense for something so new. I honestly don't know, because I was just so into falling in love with you that I didn't see anything else. But that's just the way we came together, Fallon. Right or wrong, that's what we did to each other. Now I wish—"

"That we hadn't?" she interrupted.

"No, I'll never wish that. But I do wish I'd found a better way to handle things after you were injured. Because maybe if I had, we might not be at this point now." He shook his head. "And I can't figure out why you're always resisting me, Fallon. If I thought that by backing off a few weeks, or even a few months, things would be better at the end of it, I would. But I know that if I do back off, you'll slip away altogether."

"That's what I want to do, James. What I've been telling you all along."

"Is it really, Fallon? Because one minute you're telling me to leave you alone, and the next you're falling into my arms. Oh, I know you're fighting it when you do. I can see it, feel it. But you do fall. Which makes me wonder why you push yourself away then fall right back."

"We have this attraction level," she started to explain, then stopped. "I won't deny that because we both know it's there. But why isn't it enough that when I tell you that what's in the past is in the past, you won't believe me? That when I say I don't want to get involved with you again, you keep pushing me?"

"Because you haven't put the past in the past, Fallon. I don't even know why I believe that, but I do. Something there happened. Maybe it was when I had to choose Tyler over you, maybe it wasn't. But there's something in the past, and I just don't understand what it is, because I truly believe that you would never hold my decision to be with Tyler against me. That's not the kind of person you are."

"I don't hold it against you, never have. But there's nothing to understand," she said. "Nothing at all."

"Fallon, I just want…" He stopped. This was pointless. She looked miserable, he felt totally drained. And all he'd wanted was a nice evening out. Nice dinner, nice conversation. And look what he'd turned it into. "Do you remember that night we went to Ming's? You ordered the dumplings, I ordered the scallops, and we both got…"

"Chicken nuggets," she said, the smile creeping back to her face. "Mine in a clear broth, yours in a lemon sauce. And Ming kept insisting we had what we'd ordered. And the rice was…"

"Crunchy."

"Ming said it was supposed to be crunchy."

"I was on call. It was the only place close to the hospital. I mean, this was our first date. I'd have loved taking you out to a nice restaurant, but…"

"But duty called, and you left me sitting there alone, with Ming watching over me like a hawk, getting insulted when I slowed down my eating. And the food was horrible. It tasted like dirty dishwater, not that I've ever tasted dirty dishwater. But if I had, I think that's what Ming's food tasted like."

James laughed. "I did come back, though."

"An hour later. I sat there one whole hour, and Ming got so worried that I was alone he sent his teenage nephew over to keep me company…a kid who was plugged into his music, who spent most of that hour drumming rhythms on the table and droning the words to whatever he was listening to. It wasn't the best first date I've ever had."

"But the most original. And I did make it up to you the next night, when I wasn't on call." He'd cooked, they'd stayed in, listened to good music, danced, watched the dawn come up together, surprised that the night had escaped them so quickly. A night like he'd hoped for tonight. But he'd been wrong, and maybe it *was* time to quit pushing her. Maybe it *was* time to simply stand back and see what happened. For the life of him, though, he wasn't sure he could. Wasn't sure he knew how.

"That was a nice night," she agreed.

The night he'd known he loved her. Oh, he'd thought that at first sight, had been pretty sure of it after she'd been so good about the awful debacle at Ming's. But on their second night he'd known for sure, and hadn't even been surprised how hard he'd fallen, and how fast. Because it was Fallon and she was…everything.

Later, when he'd dropped her off at the bus station to send her back to White Elk, it had felt like someone was kicking him in the gut. Seeing her step up on the bus, her hesitant little stop on the top step, turning around and smiling at him…her face in the window as the bus had pulled away… Damn, he loved her. Loved her then, loved her more now, even though she was fighting him. Because she still was everything. And he missed her so badly, even when she was sitting right across the table from him, he ached. There was such a distance now. "Would you dance with me, Fallon?" he asked impulsively. "Nothing intended but a dance." Truth was, he wanted her in his arms, needed her there, needed to close that distance. Any way would do.

He didn't expect her to say yes, though. For a moment he wished he hadn't asked inasmuch as he didn't know if he could bear the rejection. Yet when he looked at her for an answer, she smiled, nodded.

"Just one," she said. "*Only* a dance. Nothing else."

He wasn't sure why, but he knew the heavens were smiling on him as he led her to the dance floor and a fairly brisk tune turned into a mellow, slow one. She didn't meld easily into his arms, and at first he could feel every tense muscle in her body fighting against him. Her dance flow was stiff, her breathing shallow in his ear. But she felt good in his arms. And that's all he concentrated on for the next three minutes as the song played on, and the two of them, in an embrace, swayed to its rhythm.

About halfway through, Fallon began to relax into him. Her sway to the music mellowed. Her head dropped to his shoulder, a sigh escaped her lips, and for a moment they were the couple they'd been at the beginning. No cares, no worries. Simply two people falling in love and enjoying the moment.

It was a song and a mood that could have gone on much longer. For ever. But all too soon it was over, and he was leading her off the dance floor, grateful for one dance and quite aware he should not push his luck and ask for another.

"That was nice," she said, but the stiffness returned to her voice the instant she sat back down. "I enjoyed it, thank you."

It was a formal thank-you, not an easy one. And that's when he knew that it was time to step away. For good? He didn't know. Didn't want it to be. But he didn't want to burn all his bridges now, and he was afraid he was getting close to that. So, yes, it was time to move on, and hope that space would be the healer, or at least the eye-opener. Pray that when she opened her eyes she'd see him standing there, waiting for her, wanting her. Because the alternative scared him...opening her eyes and being glad he was gone. "Look, Fallon, I have some news. I thought about waiting until later, but..." He shrugged, a gesture reminiscent of Tyler's. "I may have found a place for Tyler and me to live. It was offered, I have the keys so I can look at it whenever I want."

"Really?" She nearly choked with surprise.

"Even if I take the place, Tyler needs some balance for the holidays, so I wouldn't do anything until after New Year. And if we leave, you'll get your life back. I know we've been disruptive, and you've hated it. So this way—"

"I haven't hated it," she interrupted. "And it's only been a few days. I thought..." She paused, seemed to re-think what she was about to say then forced a smile. "I hope Tyler will find some children to play with. He needs them."

For an instant she'd seemed like she wanted to stop them leaving. At least, that's what he'd been hoping for. But Fallon, true to who she was now, simply built the wall a little higher around herself, and stayed there through the dinner's main course and halfway through the dessert. Stiff conversation, and very little of it, took up the space between them. Until a commotion at one of the tables near the window caught their attention.

Fallon whirled around to look, knew immediately what it was. So did James, who launched himself from his chair without a thought. Like well-trained sprinters, they were across the room in a second, with James going into action first and Fallon doing what she always did, what she was born to do—taking control of the situation. "Please, everybody, move back. We need some room here."

She looked down at the man who was sprawled on the floor, and gasped. Walt Graham. Former obstetrician at the hospital, someone she knew well. "Aspirating?" she asked James.

He shook his head gravely. "Don't think so."

Bracing herself for the worst, Fallon flagged over a man she recognized. "We're in a white pick-up truck, parked in the last row." She bent, grabbed the keys from James's pants pockets then tossed them to the man. "There's a medical bag behind the seat. We need it urgently."

The man didn't question her. Didn't even blink. He simply turned and ran from the restaurant as Fallon pushed the line of observers even farther back from Walt. For his sake, she didn't want them witnessing this. He deserved his privacy, and dignity. And there was nothing dignified about collapsing in public this way.

"What do you need?" Angela Blanchard called, running up to her.

"More privacy?"

"I can do that. Anything else?" Angela, sister of Dinah Ramsey, looked down at Walt and gasped. In the early days of her pregnancy he'd been her doctor. "Did he choke on the food?" she asked.

Fallon leaned over, whispered, "I don't think so. James is trying to figure it out, and so far all I've done is manage to get the crowd pushed back. Call Eric, tell him we need transport up here. Helicopter, if he or Neil can manage it. Ambulance, if not. Tell him it's Walt."

"It's that serious?" Angela asked, on the verge of tears.

"He's not conscious, but James hasn't started CPR, so that's a good thing."

Angela nodded, turned and ran to her staff. Within seconds the guests of the restaurant were being moved even further back, while Angela was making arrangements to have Walt taken to the hospital.

Fallon dropped to her knees alongside James. "Walt," she whispered. "It's Fallon. Don't worry, I'm here to take care of you." Her fingers went automatically to his pulse. Weak, but there.

"What?" she asked James, who was trying to assess Walt's pupils without the proper equipment.

"Diabetic coma, I'm guessing. I can smell it on his breath, that fruitiness."

"I've sent someone for your medical bag. It'll be here in a minute. And I've arranged to have him transported to the hospital."

"Already?"

She shrugged. "It's what I do."

"So, you know this guy? Do you know anything about his medical history?"

"He's a part-time doctor at the hospital. Retired, mostly. But he'll come back when we need him, if we can find him. And as far as I know, he's very healthy. At least, that's what I'm assuming as he's spent the better part of the last half-year hiking around in the mountains."

"This is Walter Graham?" James asked, unbuttoning Walt's shirt. "I've heard about him."

"He's Santa Claus."

"What?"

"On the Christmas train. He's Santa Claus. That's probably why he's back in town. The train starts running in few days, and it has to have Santa Claus on it. Walt's been Santa for twenty-five years now."

"Your bag," a winded man said, running up behind them. He looked down at Walt. "He delivered all three of my children. Is he going to be OK?"

"We're trying," Fallon said, more for Walt than the man. "We're really trying." But trying wasn't good enough, and if this did turn out to be a diabetic problem he needed to be in an intensive care unit, with drugs they wouldn't have out in the field. Question was, would they be quick enough to save his life?

While James listened to Walt's chest, Fallon took a blood-pressure reading. Choked in surprise. Took it again. "Walt," she gasped, even though the man clearly could not hear her. "Did you know you're hypertensive?"

"What is it?" James asked.

"Two-twenty over one-sixty."

James let out a small whistle. "I don't suppose you'd know if he was being treated for it?"

"Knowing Walt, he wasn't. He's as stubborn as they come. Good at demanding things from his patients and nagging at them until they do it, but apparently not so good when it comes to taking care of himself."

"Well, it goes with his condition. Not unusual in diabetes, especially if he's not been treated."

"Look, James, you stay here. I'm going out to the parking lot and see if I can see anybody coming…an ambulance, a helicopter." It was much too soon, she knew, but she couldn't just kneel here doing nothing. "I'll be right back." She stood, and practically ran over a wall of a man standing behind her. Handsome man, sun-bronzed complexion, dark brown hair. A real breath-taker for some lucky woman. "Sorry," she said, stepping around him.

"I'm a doctor," he said, his voice almost a whisper. "If you need some help here."

She pointed to James. "Dr. Galbraith there might need you. Check with him, and I'll be right back." She wondered who the doctor was. Didn't think he was on staff at the hospital. Pretty sure he didn't live in White Elk. Probably one of the many here on holiday, and she was glad he was there to assist James, if necessary. Because she needed to be in the parking lot, ready to direct the rescue crew the minute they arrived. Ready to expedite that end of the emergency.

On her way out the door, her phone rang. Dinah Ramsey, according to caller ID. "Eric said his ETA is less than five minutes," she said breathlessly. "Neil's gone to Emergency to get things set up. Is it true, that it might be a diabetic coma?"

"James thinks so. And hypertensive as a collateral condition. His wife took good care of him all those years, then when she died he went to pieces in more ways than one." The loss of true love was something she understood.

Lights in the sky, followed by the whir of the engine caught her attention. Caused her heart to pound harder, her breaths to strangle in her throat. No matter how hard she tried to keep herself calm, it didn't always happen. "I think…" Deep breath. "I think I see him. Is Eric flying?" She made herself focus on how she *was not* going up in that helicopter, willed her heart to stop its galloping, demanded her breathing go back to normal.

"That's his helicopter. He finally took the plunge and he's trying it out before the hospital makes the purchase. Look, Fallon, tell James that Tyler is fine with me and the girls. We've had pizza, and I've got them all settled in, watching a movie. As I have an idea this is going to be a late one, why don't you let him stay here tonight? That way you and James won't have to worry about him."

The way Dinah talked, it was almost as if she and James were parents and Tyler was their child. It was a nice image, just not the real one. "I'll let James know. And if he wants to do anything different, I'll have him call you. Gotta go." She ran to the edge of the parking lot and watched the helicopter land in a field at the end of it. Before she could run to greet its pilot, Eric had jumped out and was halfway across the grass, running as fast as he could, carrying an armload of supplies. "More in the chopper," he yelled as he passed Fallon. "Grab the stretcher if you can."

She grabbed the stretcher, a lightweight frame, and a bag full of miscellaneous supplies and ran right back to the lodge, where Eric was already hooking Walt up to a heart monitor, James was readying an oxygen set-up, and the unknown doctor was taking vital signs. As soon as she got there, she wiggled her way in next to James to begin the IV prep.

"He's coming round," James said, as Walt started fighting the oxygen mask, thrashing about, trying to strike out at his rescuers.

"Walt," Fallon said in her sternest voice. "Listen to me. We're trying to help you. Please don't fight us."

Walt opened his eyes, but they didn't focus.

"Do you understand? We're trying to help you."

His eyes moved slowly until they locked on Fallon, and

whether or not he understood her words was anybody's guess, but once he saw her, he settled right down.

"I'm afraid he's going to start thrashing again once I stick him to get the IV in," she whispered to James.

The other doctor responded. "How about I do that while you keep talking to him? He seems to calm down when he hears your voice, so hold his other hand, make sure he keeps his mask on."

"As soon as you get the IV started, we're going to take him down to the hospital," Eric said. "Mark can ride with me, and you two can get back to doing whatever you were doing." He smiled. "A date, wasn't it?"

"Dinner," Fallon corrected him. "That's what we were doing. Just *dinner*. And wouldn't you rather have someone you know with you on the transport...James." She wouldn't fly, wasn't sure she ever could again, but James would. And after being in his arms, after that one dance, she was ready to get some space from him.

"Mark Anderson," the other doctor said by way of introduction. "And Eric knows me. He and I...and Neil Ranard were colleagues back in California." He held down Walt's arm while James located the vein and sank the IV. Within seconds the bag was hooked up, and all three men were in the process of getting Walt strapped to the stretcher. Once that deed was done, James, Eric and Mark rushed him out the door, leaving Fallon standing in the middle of the dining room alone as all the diners still stood off to the side, watching.

"You OK?" Angela asked, rushing to Fallon's side as she prepared to leave.

"Sure. Tired, but OK."

"That was amazing, what you and James did. I admire all of you...my sister, Eric. I mean, I come here and cook every night, and you...you do something that counts."

"Cooking counts," Fallon said, suddenly realizing she was on the verge of total exhaustion. "Without the cooks of the world, those of us who burn water would starve."

"Who was the other doctor?" Angela asked. "I haven't seen him before."

Fallon tried to remember his name. "Rick. Or, Mark. I think I heard him say he was from California, but I was talking to Walt at the time, trying to reassure him."

"He's going to be OK, isn't he? I mean, I was thinking that if you and James hadn't been here when he collapsed…"

As the helicopter lifted off, and she watched it makes its way skyward, Fallon's head went light and she took a staggering step backwards. "I think I need to go home," she said. "I'll call you as soon as I hear anything about Walt."

"Can I drive you?"

"I think James is waiting for me. At the truck. He was going to help get Walt loaded into the helicopter then come and get me. But thanks." The two exchanged hugs, and as Fallon was about to pull away from Angela, James stepped up behind her.

"James *is* waiting for you. And he's taking you straight home and putting you to bed." Angela took that as the hint to leave them alone as James slid his arm around Fallon's waist to support her. Never had anything felt so good. At any other time she would have struggled to stand on her own, but this was the second time James had practically carried her home, and this was the second time she had been willing to let him do it.

"Tyler's with Dinah and the twins. Spending the night, if that's OK with you."

As the two of them strolled across the parking lot to the truck, she leaned into him more and more, until he was practically holding up her full weight. "Eric mentioned that. I told him it was fine with me. Look, Fallon, I think maybe I should carry you."

"No, I'll make it…" As long as he was there to help her. "I don't have my full stamina back and I think my little adrenalin surge has worn off. But I can walk to the truck."

Which she did. And she even walked into the cabin on her own. But made it only as far as the couch, where she collapsed, promising herself she'd rest a minute or two before she climbed the stairs to her bedroom. She had to get up those stairs because she was feeling too vulnerable, too cozy. She wanted to shut a door between them. Wanted to put up a physical barrier that would block out everything she was fighting to give in to. She and James together, upstairs. Weak thoughts attributed to a tired body. Something she had to remember. "Thanks for dinner," she said, as she pushed herself up off the couch. "I'm sorry it didn't turn out better."

"Well, except for the first half-hour when you were so nervous, and the last half hour when Walt collapsed, it wasn't all that bad."

Fallon laughed. "Always the optimist, aren't you? Seeing the glass half-full, not half-empty."

"But it is half-full. Although I'll admit, when I asked you to dance, I was pretty sure it was going to be empty."

"But I danced."

"That, you did. And I'm wondering why."

She looked up at him, sighed. Attempted a smile. "Because you wanted to. I'm not an ogre, James. I do want to be your friend, if we can find a way to work that out."

"Friend? That's all?" He shook his head, sucked in a frustrated breath and let it out slowly. "I can't keep doing this, Fallon. Can't keep hoping. It's getting more and more exhausting for me. And right now the only thing on my mind is how much I want to carry you up those stairs, which is why I'm going to leave. I've decided to buy Emoline Putters's house sight unseen. Maybe move in as soon as the day after Christmas. Because I need to get out of here. Need to get Tyler out of here and leave you to whatever it is you want to be left to."

The words she'd been wanting to hear. But hearing them didn't make her feel any better. If anything, she felt worse. Afraid. Alone. She couldn't let him see that, though, or he wouldn't leave. So she braved up, squared her shoulders, forced a smile. "You're right. That's what you need to do. It'll be best for everyone."

"And that's it?"

"What else should there be, James? This was never a permanent arrangement. You were always going to leave, and now it's official." Her brave front was slipping, but she didn't want him to see that. "So, in the meantime, if you hear anything about Walt, let me know. Yell it from the bottom of the stairs, though. I don't want you coming up."

"Be honest with me, Fallon. Is that because if I did get to the top, you wouldn't send me back down?"

She couldn't lie to him. Dear God, she wished she could. That would make it easier. But she couldn't. "If you climbed those stairs, I wouldn't send you back down." She turned away and started walking upstairs, wondering, for a moment, if they could have just one night…one more night. Make it simple, be clear about it. Wake up in each other's arms for one last time. Say the final goodbye to the part of their lives that desperately needed closure, and start a new chapter, separately. Her list of reasons sounded good to a weary mind. So why not? James would understand what it was about and maybe it would help him move on. Help her move on.

She could do this. And it didn't mean she was giving in. It meant that she was finally putting it to rest. Closure. Yes, that was it. She was seeking closure. Of course, there was the real possibility that in the morning, when her head was clear, she'd regret her decision, and see her list for what it was…a pathetic attempt to live in the past, to hang onto a part of that past she couldn't have now. She turned to invite him up, but he was already gone. And she didn't go after him.

"He's doing well. Grumpy, but otherwise in remarkably good condition for what he suffered last night."

"Huh?" Fallon looked up at James through a hazy stupor. She hadn't slept at all last night. She'd tossed and turned, paced, fixed herself hot milk, read a magazine, gone over files for the new hospital, and admonished herself for what she'd almost done every second her head hadn't been full of something else. She would have slept with him. Made love, and quite possibly would have been making love again right this very minute. So this morning she wasn't up to facing him. More than that, she wasn't up to facing herself.

"Walt Graham. He's grumpy…"

"He was always grumpy," she said, twisting away from James. He was standing over her, she was sitting at the breakfast bar, pretending to eat a carton of yogurt. There was no way she could twist far enough away from him to forget what she'd wanted to do. "Gentle soul inside, grumpy on the outside."

"He wants to be Santa. Says he'll check himself out of the hospital and do what he wants to do."

Fallon managed a laugh, in spite of her glum mood.

"And that's what he'll do, if there's any way he can get himself into his Santa suit and hoist himself up on that train."

"That's what Eric said, too. We had coffee together a while ago, and he said Walt could bellow all he wanted, but he was grounded this year."

"You had coffee with Eric?"

"And Neil and Gabby, and the rest of the doctors. Staff meeting, actually. Bright and early. We talked about expanding the hospital by another new staff member."

She hadn't known, hadn't heard him leave. And here her thoughts had been full of sweet morning love. Well, now, if she didn't just feel like an idiot! Glad, though, that James hadn't been privy to the tumultuous thoughts that had kept her awake all night.

"And I stopped by the Ramseys' to see Tyler for a few minutes. He was busy making snow angels. He said he still wants to build a snowman with you, and do all that Christmas shopping you promised him. And he doesn't want you forgetting that." James chuckled. "He's enjoying the attention of two lovely ladies, though. I've been told Paige and Pippa have both declared their undying love for him, and they don't want him going home, *ever*. But my little Casanova took me aside and told me he wants to come back here with you."

Suddenly, her bad mood melted away. "He does?" she asked, finally mellow enough to look him straight in the eye. "Are you sure?"

"He likes you, Fallon. Like father, like son."

"Are you on duty, or can you come with us to build that snowman?"

"On for the morning, off for the rest of the day."

"Then how about Tyler and I go shopping for ornaments, and after you're home we start on the snowman and maybe drag the tree into the house. He's really anxious to put it up, you know."

His face darkened. "I have an emergency hearing this afternoon. My attorney got the temporary custody papers filed, and the judge wants to hear the case immediately."

"That's fast!"

He nodded. "I'm not sure what to make of it, but he wants Tyler there with me. So maybe we can get to the snowman or the tree afterwards."

It was all beginning to happen. James getting custody of Tyler. Tyler and James starting their new life together. She was happy for them. Truly happy for them. But sad for herself because she already felt left out. It's what she wanted, but she didn't have to like it, didn't have to like the feeling it left her with. Still, she was glad for James because he did deserve some happiness.

And her…getting what she wanted ached so bad she wanted to curl up in a tight, little ball and stay that way. She missed James and he wasn't even gone. So, how was she to survive this? How was she to make it through the next days without giving herself away to him? Because the tears welling behind her eyes right now would surely give her away. And she couldn't let him see that. Not now, not ever.

CHAPTER NINE

"AND you have no knowledge of her whereabouts?" Judge Stanley asked James.

"She may live in Arizona or New Mexico. But Tyler doesn't know, and as she didn't leave me any forwarding information, I don't know either. My attorney and I are working on that, though. And I've had an investigator looking for her for a while."

"But the blood tests match? And the DNA?" He shuffled through a stack of papers, looking through a tiny pair of reading glasses that balanced precariously on the end of his nose.

"No doubts," James said. "He's my son."

The judge nodded without looking up. "And you dated the mother for how long?"

This was beginning to make him nervous. "A few weeks. Not seriously, though."

He glanced up at James. "Seriously enough to conceive a son." Then he returned to his papers.

Bad sign. Really bad sign. He wished he could have asked Fallon to come and stand with him. Even though Jason Greene was with him, he felt alone. Tyler was sitting in the judge's office, under the watchful eye of a court clerk, and here he was, doing something he'd never even considered would happen to him. He was asking the judge to take the first legal steps in granting him sole custody of his son. It was good, but he missed Fallon being involved. It wasn't her fight, though. And he knew he had to get used to not having her around because, as of an hour ago, he'd agreed to buy Emoline's house. Which meant he was doing what Fallon wanted all along…moving on.

So why involve her in this, when in a few more days she wouldn't be involved in anything in his life? He did hope, though, that she'd stay involved with Tyler. Tyler loved her.

"Seriously enough to conceive a son," he said back to the judge.

"What happens when you get to a permanent custody hearing and the boy's mother fights you?"

"I fight her back. After all, I'm not the one who keeps abandoning our son. I'd say that's a pretty good argument."

The judge looked up again, but this time took off his glasses. "What you're asking to do here, Doctor, is the start of something with a very serious consequence. You realize that, don't you?"

"What I realize is my son needs a stable life. I can give that to him, but his mother cannot. If she wants visitation rights, we can work that out because I think it's important that Tyler has a relationship with his mother. But I'll do everything in my power, spend every cent I have if that's what it takes, to make sure he spends the rest of his child-hood with me."

"Well, according to the court report, he's a difficult child…behavioral problems of some undiagnosed sort," the judge continued. "I know you're a pediatrician, well aware of what adjustments might have to be made for the boy. But are you prepared to deal with that every day until the permanent custody is established and, perhaps, for the duration of his childhood, if that's the way it works out? Deal with it as a father?"

"It's the *father* in me who wants to take care of his son. The *father* who loves that little boy more than life itself, and wants to give him the kind of home he deserves. That's who you see right now, and I'm fully prepared to deal with his problems. Although once he has someone he can count on, once he knows he's not going to be abandoned every few months, his behavioral issues will disappear. And that's the pediatrician speaking as a professional."

Outside, in the corridor, Fallon shut the door to the hearing room and dropped down onto the wooden bench there in the hall. OK, so she really didn't need to be here, had promised herself that she wouldn't come. But she had anyway. And she'd been listening to the arguments and discussions for the past twenty minutes, standing there with the door opened barely a crack, ready to spring in and testify on James's behalf, if he needed it. But he didn't need it, and the tears streaming down her cheeks were the proof of that. Tyler was on the verge of a new life now, and she was so happy for the both of them. If only she could have been part of that arrangement.

"Why didn't you come in?" He'd known she was there. Had seen her peeking in.

Fallon, still facing her car, with her key in the door, sucked in a sharp breath. "I didn't know if you wanted me there. And I didn't want to intrude."

He took her by the shoulder and spun her around. "There's no place in my life I don't want you, Fallon. But I don't know how to get you back in my life the way I want you." With the snowflakes brushing her face as they fluttered to the ground, and her eyes so wide and questioning, she was the most beautiful woman he'd ever seen. So much so she nearly took his breath away. "And I didn't ask you to testify for me because…." He brushed a snowflake off her cheek. Wanted to kiss her so badly it stung. "Because it's so difficult, Fallon. Wanting you, knowing I can't have you."

"But I would have testified. If you'd asked I would have."

"I know you would, but this distance between us…it shows. People can see it, see the tension. And I was afraid the judge might wonder why the woman Tyler and I are living with would appear so standoffish. So I couldn't risk it." Mentally, he braced himself not to step forward, not to cross that invisible barrier she had up around herself. "Sometimes, Fallon, it's not about you. I'm sorry, but I was afraid you could hurt my chances."

Tears immediately sprang to her eyes. "You're right," she said, turning back to the car. "It's not about me."

Damn, he hated himself. Hated this situation. Hated it that he couldn't risk pulling her into his arms to shield her from the world she feared. "I'm sorry," he whispered, his voice nearly breaking with agony. "I didn't mean to hurt you."

Still facing the car, she said, "I know you didn't. I'm the one who hurts you, the one who should be apologizing."

What kind of man would let the woman he loved hurt so badly and simply stand there and watch it? The worst kind. The answer sat bitterly in his heart. *The worst kind.* He was at breaking point. "Fallon," he said, his voice turning rough. "Turn around, look at me."

She didn't. So he stepped around and physically wedged himself between her and the car door, and when she started to back away from him, he took hold of her arm, stopped her. Then, when she started to pull back the way he knew she would do, started to tilt her head toward the ground, he stopped her. Placed his hand under her chin and tipped her face toward his, fully expecting her to pull away, to literally run away.

But, she didn't, and that surprised him. Fallon stood there, meeting him eye to eye, and allowed him everything he needed for the first moments. But it wasn't enough. He knew that, so did she. Then as if some gusty mountain wind blew her right into his arms, she was there, her arms snaked around his neck, her body pressed so close to his he felt every one of her curves, even through her bulky winter clothing. It didn't take but a second for him to respond to the need tearing at him, right there in the public parking lot of the White Elk Town Hall, so aroused he couldn't think straight. It didn't take but another second for his lips to claim hers…hard, demanding. They'd always been vigorous in their passion, and this kiss was no exception. But it was *her* tongue forcing its way into his mouth now, *her* tongue exploring the warm, sensitive contours, *her* tongue causing him to groan like no man had a right to groan in a public place.

Had the chill wind not been blowing swirls of snow around their ankles, he would have thought he was hallucinating. But as the cold crept up his leg and joined with the fire she was igniting in him, he was snapped into the realization that he couldn't do this. This time he was the one who had to pull away because if he didn't, Fallon would retreat and, perhaps, this time she might never come back because he was, indeed, moving on. Besides, what he wanted from her was so much more than a feverish kiss in a wintry parking lot. So he broke loose, pulled back, hated doing it. Dear God, he hated doing it. But what choice did he have? It wasn't the little campaigns he wanted to win with her.

"I...I shouldn't have done that," she stammered, raising her hand to her lips.

Already they were red and swollen from the encounter. And so inviting it was all he could do to keep himself from claiming them once more. "You're right," he said, backing away from her. "We shouldn't have. Look, I've got to go back inside and get Tyler. Why don't we meet at the mercantile and do that shopping you've been promising him then we can go put up the tree?" Unless she didn't want them in her house any more. That was the question that hung in the air between them for the next moment.

"What we did shouldn't ruin his holiday," she said. "I know you're getting ready to move, but I think you should stay until after Christmas so he can have some sense of belonging. It's only for a few more days, and..." She paused, grappled for the right words. "And we won't do that again. For Tyler's sake, we can't. Agreed?"

"Agreed," he said. Agreed, but not sorry about what he'd done.

Fallon forced a difficult smile. "Good. Then I'll meet you at the mercantile in a while."

Which she did. Fighting with herself every step of the way. Why had she kissed him like that? And there was no mistaking what had happened. He'd approached and she'd taken full advantage. Like a woman possessed. Well, it was a good thing they'd be gone after the holidays because it was clear that the best intentions meant nothing. Where James was concerned, the only way to deal with him the way she needed to was to completely remove him from her life. Otherwise... She cringed, thinking about what tagged along on the end of that otherwise. She was so close to the edge and ready to topple. Make no mistake, she was the one standing right there, ready to give herself the shove that would send her plummeting. And all it would take was such a little shove.

"The star goes at the top," she said, handing it up to James, who was balanced precariously on a wobbly stepladder. Tyler was busy below, hanging the several dozen ornaments he'd chosen. No theme to this tree other than fun. Tyler definitely showed a preference for cartoon-character ornaments, while her taste ran more to snowmen and Santas and angels. James didn't have a preference, so he concentrated on the lights and chose strands of all different colors, lights that twinkled. All in all, it was turning out to be a rather amazing mix of gaiety, and after the first hour of stringing up decorations, the trio put the project on pause long enough to take advantage of the fresh snow outside, where James instructed Fallon and Tyler in the fine art of snowman-building.

Naturally, they all had their own variations on a theme, Fallon making more of a snow princess, adorned in an old sequined shawl she hadn't worn in years, while Tyler definitely went for something more in his own image and size. James, on the other hand, had a secret project going, and insisted that Fallon and Tyler were not to come around to the south end of the cabin until he called them.

"Think we should sneak around there and see if we can have a peek?" she whispered to Tyler.

"Maybe he'll get mad at me," Tyler said, on the verge of turning sullen after a long afternoon filled with so many fun things.

Poor child. He deserved time to be carefree, time to be a little boy who didn't have such deep worries on his mind. "Why would that make him angry?" she asked.

"I have to do what he says. That's the way it is."

"What happens if you don't? What do you think he might do?"

Big tears started to roll down Tyler's face. "Make me go live with someone else."

"Like your mother made you come live with James when you didn't know him?"

He nodded.

"Do you want to stay here?"

He nodded again.

"Well, your dad...*James* wants you to stay here."

"Do you, too?"

"Of course I do. I want us to be best friends."

"You're not going to be my mom?"

This was getting too complicated. And she truly didn't know what to say because Tyler would see just how broken up she was about this, and she didn't want him to feel like it was his fault that he and James would be moving out. Thankfully, James interrupted at just the right moment.

"You two about ready for the big unveiling?" James shouted from the other side of the house.

She held out her hand to take Tyler's, and he grabbed hold and clung like she was his lifeline. "Remember how big heads on snowmen are what makes them fall over?"

"Un-huh."

"Think this one will have a big head?"

The answer to that awaited them just around the corner, where James had constructed a large snowman, with a huge head. One he was fighting to keep on top.

"It's going to fall!" Tyler squealed, breaking away from Fallon and running straight to James. Actually, more like straight into James. Which sent James falling backwards, causing one huge snowman head to fall on top of both of them.

"Want me to show you how to make a better one?" Tyler asked innocently, as he poked his head out of the snow.

A better snowman, a better life…Tyler had so many things to show them, if either of them were open enough to learn the lessons of a child.

"That's what he said?"

Fallon nodded. Settling into the couch, with a mug of hot chocolate in hand, she tucked her feet up under herself and stared at the Christmas tree. It was a mess, and it was also the most beautiful tree she'd ever seen. "He wanted to know if I was going to be his mom."

"And you said?"

"Nothing. I didn't know what to say. I think it's pretty clear he doesn't want to go back to his real mom, though. Probably not even for visitation, if the court decided to allow that."

James shut his eyes, dropped his head back against the chair. "It's always going to be in his mind, isn't it? Even if he never goes back to her, if he stays here with me until he's an adult, and lives a normal life, he's never going to get over what she's done to him."

"But you can help him deal with it. It's not easy, but you can teach him to be a strong little boy. And, James, he'll learn to trust you. Once he's certain of consistency in his life, something he knows he can count on, he'll trust you."

"Did anybody ever help you learn to deal with it?"

She shook her head, too close to tears to speak.

"Talk to me, Fallon. Tell me what I need to know, what you need to say. It's driving me crazy. I see it there, see it in your eyes, and don't understand it. And I want to."

"What I need to say? Like, I was thrown away just like Tyler was? To be honest, James, that's all there is to say.

It hurts, and you never stop wondering why the ones who should love you the most don't." She drew in a ragged breath, swiped away a tear. "But you can help him get past that. And that's what he needs the most. Someone fighting for him, someone who loves him so much he'll never give up."

"The way I love you, Fallon. The way I won't give up, even though you keep trying to push me away?"

She thrust out her hand to stop him. "Don't, James. I keep telling you, over and over, that I can't deal with it any more."

"Why?" he asked. "You owe me that much. Tell me why, Fallon. The truth… I deserve to know what's keeping us apart. Because, I can't, for the life of me, figure it out, and I want to. And I won't move on until I know."

She laid her hands across her belly, could almost feel the barrenness under her fingertips. There was no fight left in her any more. James was right. "I guess you do deserve that closure, don't you?" She drew in a deep breath, braced herself. Felt surprisingly calm about it. Now that the moment had arrived, it seemed surreal, finally knowing that this would end it…end the relationship, end them, end the dreams. Permanently. But she loved this man more than anything she'd ever known, and she owed him this one, final truth. "I suppose the simple answer would be that one of my surgeries was a hysterectomy. I can't have children. Can't give you all those children we'd planned on having."

He arched his eyebrows in surprise, but didn't get overly emotional. "And you didn't tell me?"

"No. Because I…because I…" The words were so difficult to find. She'd rehearsed them a million times all these months, known exactly what she would say when the time came. But now she couldn't find them. "I was afraid, I suppose."

"A hysterectomy doesn't matter, Fallon. We can deal with that! If we want children, we can adopt. Or concentrate on raising the one I hope we're about to get custody of."

"I know that, and for a while that's what I told myself. Tell James about the hysterectomy and leave it at that. But the hysterectomy is the simple part, James. It's what came before." She wouldn't look at him for this. Couldn't look at what she knew she would see on his face. "Before we... before the plane crash...I discovered I was pregnant."

"Oh, my God!" he whispered. The emotion was rising now. He wasn't holding it back. "Fallon, I don't...don't know what to say..." Anguished words. So much pain in them already. The pain she'd never wanted to cause.

"It's not what you need to say, James. It's what I need to say, what I've needed to say for such a long time, and couldn't. I knew about my pregnancy for a few weeks before the plane crash, and I kept it to myself. You were under so much stress at the time with your job, and I wanted to find the perfect time to tell you. I had these visions of what that perfect time would be like, but you were struggling so much, always on edge, that I kept putting it off, telling myself I'd tell you tomorrow, or the day after that. But it never seemed like the right time. I should have just come right out and told you, but in the back of my mind I saw something so nice. Not like what happened with my mother, who never even knew who my father was.

"Also, I was nervous because we really hadn't been together very long. We'd had a couple of intense months and I knew we had deep feelings, but I think I was afraid that we might be mistaking physical passion for the real

thing. Whatever the case, I kept it to myself, always thinking that we had tomorrow. And I'm so sorry I did."

"So am I. I would have liked knowing. Liked to experience it with you. But I do understand your confusion."

She turned her head to look at him. "See, that's the
thing. Maybe you think you understand right now, but
what happens after it's sunk in, after you're not in shock?
After you've had time to think about what I did...to you.
James, I don't want you being so nice to me. I don't deserve
it. Don't want it!"

"You want me to be angry because you miscarried in
the plane crash? It wasn't your fault, Fallon! You're right, I
may be angry after I've absorbed that you weren't ready to
tell me, but I'd never blame you for how it turned out."

"The thing is, James, I didn't miscarry. I came through
the crash, badly injured, with my pregnancy intact.
Had so many surgeries afterwards. The surgeries, the
anesthesia…"

"No," he choked. "I don't understand. You didn't miscarry and you still didn't tell me?"

Now she saw the anger. It was awful, she hated it, but
this was the way it had to be. And every time he looked
at her, she'd be the reminder of something bad, something
filled with indescribable pain. The secret he couldn't forgive. "How could I? I was fighting to stay alive, fighting
to keep my baby alive, and you…"

"I was busy with Tyler." With this his anger turned to
agony. "I thought you were strong enough, took you for
granted, and I wasn't there the way you needed me to
be."

"Tyler needed you. I always understood that. You'd told
me he was going through a hard time. And he was…was
my baby's brother. I couldn't let you divide yourself!

"And, James, I really thought that I would tell you about

our baby when my physical condition improved, when you weren't fighting so many battles. But nothing got better. I had so many complications, and I knew that if you found out what I was going through, you'd be with me, stay with me, never leave my side. You couldn't do that, though. Don't you see? I couldn't take you away from Tyler. He wasn't part of me but he was part of you…part of our child. And I was a mother too. A mother fighting to save her baby…a mother with a baby inside her who needed her to fight for him the way you needed to fight for Tyler. That's the way it had to be, James. You had to take care of Tyler, not me."

"What happened?" he choked, his voice so hoarse the words barely came out. "To the…to our baby?"

"I had our baby…stillbirth. I was just over six months along."

"Six months?" he gasped. "You were six months along and didn't tell me? How could you do that, Fallon? I had the right to know."

"You did. I always knew that, and felt so guilty. But the longer I didn't tell you, the more I didn't know how. And my lawyer… He checked in on you, told me about your situation with Tyler. You had him, he was taken away. Then you got him again… And I was so…so confused. So hurt." She drew in a steadying breath. "For the longest time I had this fantasy that our baby would be fine. That one day I'd call you to come visit us, and I'd introduce you to him. In retrospect, I know I was kidding myself about the outcome, because I did know how bad the situation was. But I'd fantasize that I'd get to the end of the pregnancy, give birth, then…

"But the other part of me, the pragmatist, knew that you were in such a dark place, and it hurt me. I truly didn't want to burden you with more, and I'd convinced myself that not telling you was protecting you from even more pain.

"Then when my mind started to clear up, I felt so… guilty. Knew I should have told you even then. But it was too late. The doctor told me the odds of my baby surviving were overwhelmingly slim, and that my odds of survival were almost none if I somehow managed to go to term, or even close to it. Still, I wasn't going to abort my baby, no matter what. I had to fight for him, and that's why I left. Why I wouldn't tell you where I was. Because if you knew…"

"You should have told me, Fallon. If your life was at risk…"

She shook her head, almost violently. "See, that's what I knew you'd say. That's what I knew I'd have to fight, and I just couldn't fight anything else. You would have won, James. You would have connected with the nurse in me, and won. I always knew that, and that's why I didn't take your calls, wouldn't let you come see me. I couldn't let you win because if you won, if you'd have convinced me to save myself and not our baby… But in the end, none of it mattered. I lost our baby anyway. And when he died I just couldn't face you. Because I know how wrong I'd been, leaving you out. You deserved to know him, to be part of him for that short time…"

"He?" James choked.

"We had a little boy." She swiped at the tears rolling down her cheeks. "And when they let me hold him, that's when I knew it was too late. That there was no going back. I cheated you of your son. You didn't get to hold him, James. You didn't get to…"

James swiped at his own tears. "Fallon, I'm so…" His words broke off. He sucked in a sharp breath. "I wouldn't have hated you. Couldn't have…"

"I hated myself, James. Don't you see? All these months I've hated myself, because I wasn't strong enough to keep him alive. Because I wasn't strong enough to tell you and fight the fight to keep our baby, if that's what I had to do. It was just easier to be alone. But you deserved better. Then, and now. I've watched you with Tyler. You're such a good father. A great father, and you love being a father. You need all those children, James. And I can't be the one to give them to you. Couldn't even be the one to give you *our* son."

"Did he have a name, Fallon? Our son, did he have a name?"

She nodded. But her lips only formed the words as her voice failed her. "James Allen Galbraith, Junior."

He didn't say anything for a while. Just sat in the chair across from her and stared out the window, for which she was grateful, because she didn't want to be in his arms, didn't want to feel the pain that would surely radiate from him, pain she had caused. So they sat in silence, for half an hour, or an hour…she didn't know. Time passed and she was too numb to feel it. But finally James cleared his throat, squared his shoulders. He stood. And she knew that once he walked out of the room, he might never come back. At least, not emotionally.

It's what she deserved. What she'd known all along would happen. But being right about it didn't make her feel any better, didn't bring her any relief.

She couldn't watch him go, however. So she shut her eyes, blocked it all out. Held her breath until she heard the door close behind him.

But it didn't close. Yet she waited. Dear God, she waited for ever, then finally opened her eyes, only to find James kneeling in front of her, the pain on his face so acute she wasn't sure either of them could get through this.

"I'm sorry," he whispered. "Fallon, I'm so sorry. What you did... I don't blame you for anything. How could I?"

"But you should. And in time you will. You should have known about the baby at the beginning so you could have celebrated the happy days with me, and at the end mourned the loss. You should have held him in your arms the way I did, and stood next to me at the grave when I... when I buried him. It was your right... He was *your* son and I took that away from you." She reached out tenderly to brush a tear from his cheek. "I was so confused..."

He took hold of her hand and kissed it. "I know you were. But, Fallon, I do understand that you did what you thought was right for me, and for Tyler. How could I ever be angry about that?"

"Don't you understand, James? I'm the one who's angry. I thought you might be, tried to convince myself you would be, but in my heart of hearts I always knew you'd forgive me. But I'm the one who's angry. So damned angry."

"At me?"

She shook her head. "At me. For not being strong enough. See, I didn't *ever* want to tell you. At first I thought that I'd never tell you, and that maybe we could get back together and simply go on. You'd never have to know. But after a while I knew that I couldn't go through with that because I can't lie to you, and not telling you the truth was lying. But I didn't want you to suffer the pain I had. Or suffer even more pain because I hadn't included you. Yet I knew that I was bound to tell you everything if we stayed together long enough, and I didn't want to hurt you. So I've been trying to push you away, James. Not because I hated you but because I loved you. But I couldn't do it. I was too...weak."

"You're not weak, Fallon. You're the strongest person

I've ever known. And what you perceive as weakness is truly strength."

"Then I hate being strong." She sniffled. "And all this time when you've said you made a mess of things…it was always me. I knew that, and I kept on letting you think it was you because I was still trying to find a way to keep my secret. I was right about one thing, though. When I told you that you don't need me, you don't. Now that you know the truth, you can move on. Start over."

"How the hell can you tell me what I need, Fallon? How the hell can you tell me to move on when you know it's breaking my heart? Everything you're telling me is breaking my heart. You are breaking my heart. But I still love you, and I don't want to walk away."

"Do you honestly think you could look at me every day for the rest of our lives and not think about what I did to you? You'll think about it for a while…days, months, years. Convince yourself that you're not angry. But then one morning, out of the blue, you'll wake up, look at me, and finally realize you hate me. And every time you'll look at me you'll remember what I did…and I can't bear that. Can't even look in a mirror at myself and not think about what I did, so how can I expect you to simply think it will go away? Right now, it's so raw, you don't know…but I've lived with it. I do know. That's why you and Tyler… You have each other and you can get on with your lives, and in time you'll both forget…"

"We'll forget you? Is that what you think? Tyler loves you, I love you, and you really believe that we'll just get over you because you tell us to?"

"Because you need to," she said, her voice breaking. "You need to, for both your sakes."

"You don't know a damn thing about what I need. Not a damn thing." He shut his eyes, trying to rein in the emotion. It wasn't sinking in yet. Oh, he understood the words. Every last, ugly one of them. And he even understood why Fallon had made the choices she had. He couldn't even begin to imagine what she'd gone through all those months, and the pain of realizing how she'd gone through it alone was nearly as bad as the pain of losing his son. So maybe she was right. Maybe in time, when it all made more sense, his feelings, his reactions would change.

But hating Fallon?

That would never happen. "It wouldn't be hate I'd have, waking up with you on that morning, Fallon. I might be angry, might want to put my fist through the wall…hell, if your walls weren't made of logs I'd put a fist through one right now. But these are things we can work through. Maybe get counseling…get it right away."

"I can't trust that, James. I can't trust…anything."

"Not even me?"

"I do trust you. That's the thing. You're the best person I've even known. The most noble. Someone who deserves a life with someone *they* can trust. And can you really say, right now, that you do trust me? Completely? Is trust your initial reaction toward me after everything I've told you?"

It wasn't. To be honest, there were so many emotions in him right now, he didn't know what he was feeling. "I need some time…"

"All the time in the world," she said, almost sounding relieved. "Because I don't have the heart to ever find out that you stopped loving me one day, and started hating me."

"I never knew you thought so little of me, Fallon," he snapped, rising from the couch.

"I don't think so little of you. But I do trust human

nature. It always comes through." And, finally, it was over. She'd pushed him away.

"You're wrong, Fallon. Dead wrong. I love you. That's all this is. I love you. But I can't do this right now." He stormed out, got to the den door, then turned around and went back to the living room. "And just so you'll know, I still love you. But you know what? I don't think you love me. You couldn't. Or else you'd have included me in this decision…not the one about our baby, but the one about ending our relationship. Because true love's about inclusion, not exclusion. And you talk about people turning their backs…about how you thought I'd turn my back on you eventually. Well, you're the one who turned your back. Not me. You."

"That's not fair! I'm doing this for you."

"Don't!" He ran an angry hand through his hair. "Pushing away someone who loves you, someone you love… You've fooled yourself into thinking you're doing this for me when, in reality, it's for you because it's the easy way out. Without me, you won't have to deal with your guilt. Not over what you did to me. But especially not over losing our baby. And that's the real guilt here, Fallon. The real anger." His voice softened. "Our baby died and you don't know what to do about it. Push me away, and you push that away from you, too. And, sweetheart, we really should be pulling together now. Now's the time we should be depending on each other to get us through it, except you won't let yourself depend on anybody, will you? And that gets to the heart of the matter. You can't let yourself depend on someone else." He shut his eyes, drew in an agonized breath. "Look, I love you, Fallon, and that's not going to change. But I love Tyler, and he needs me. I'm sorry I couldn't be the one you trusted enough to help make you whole again, but my son needs that from me now."

"And you should give it to him," she said.

"I'll give it to you, too. If you'll let me. But you have to be the one to ask, because I've done everything I can do, and I've run out of ideas. I want to marry you, want you to be Tyler's mother, but the next move is yours, Fallon. I have to fight the battles for my son, and I'll fight the battles for you...for us, too, but I have to know you'll be fighting with me, not against me. And here's the thing. It's OK to depend on someone else. I don't think you realize that, don't think you've ever allowed yourself to do it. And I'm not criticizing you for that, because I think you learned at a very young age that you couldn't depend on anyone. Tyler's learned the same thing but I'm going to teach him differently. I'm going to show him that some people will let him down, but most will not. You depend on someone, they let you down, it breaks your heart, and that's all he knows right now. All you know. Because of that you grew up strong. So strong that you became the one everybody else depended on. Then somewhere along the line you perceived any weakness in yourself as something that would let the people who depend on you down. They take you for granted...I took you for granted. But the one who takes you the most for granted is you, because you have to keep yourself at a respectable distance, especially when deep down you just want to lean on someone else for a little while. But here's the thing, Fallon. We all need to depend on others at one time or another. Hell. That's all I've been doing since Tyler came into my life."

He paused for a moment, watched her for something, anything. Saw the barriers up all around her, didn't know how to bring them down. And realized it wasn't up to him. Couldn't be up to him. Fallon had to want it. Fallon had to do it. Until she did, this was where they would stay. On that sad note, he walked over to her, bent, kissed her tenderly on forehead then straightened. "You're afraid to reach out, Fallon. Because what if you did and no one was there…like no one was there when you were a little girl? That's what this is about. Somewhere, some time, you've convinced yourself it's easier to do it alone. You stand out there by yourself as this larger-than-life woman who doesn't need anybody, someone who can handle everything by herself. But you're still that little girl who got pushed away, and you've convinced yourself that if you do it all alone, no one will hurt you. But you're hurt. And you're wrong. You can't do this alone. You shouldn't do this alone because what you've gone through… Our son died, Fallon. You didn't kill him. It wasn't your fault. No one should ever have to face something like that alone, and I'm sorry you didn't know that."

James drew in a deep breath, wanting her to respond, to say something, anything. But she wouldn't. He knew that. Knew from the expression in her eyes she was shutting him out again. And now there were no more words. It truly was up to Fallon. "I love you," he said. "I've done so many things the wrong way, so have you. But I'd never wake up some morning, look at you, and hate you. That's not what you're running away from, Fallon. And not why you're pushing me away either. I'm sorry for the choices we've both made, but there would never be a morning in my life that I wouldn't wake up knowing I loved you more than life. I trust that in myself. And I only hope you find some way to trust it in me, too. And in yourself. But if you can't…"

James withdrew to the den and shut the door, leaving Fallon alone, next to the Christmas tree. Looking up at the star on the top. "What have I done?" she whispered, pulling the blanket up to her chin, then rolling into a ball in the cushions. "What have I done?"

CHAPTER TEN

THE evening settled in bright and clear for the inaugural journey of the Christmas train, and a light dusting of snow throughout the day had made the whole event even more perfect for all the children lined up, anxiously waiting to board. For Fallon, it meant nothing, as she'd turned down numerous invitations to take the first ride. But for Tyler, and his new best friends Paige and Pippa, the all-day anticipation had been almost as bad as waiting for Christmas itself to arrive.

"Why can't she come?" Tyler whined, as he and James moved through the line to climb the steps to the train car. The train consisted of a circa 1928 steam locomotive, two cars and a bright red caboose. All restored to period, with a few exceptions meant to occupy the interests of children. Additions such as twinkling lights, music piped through the entire train and a refreshment stand specializing in hot chocolate and sugar cookies. Santa's huge throne-like chair, too. Elevated on a platform, painted in glitzy gold. For two weeks, a child's fantasy come true.

"She has other plans," James said stiffly. She was going to sit at home and order tongue depressors, or thermometers, or accomplish some other equally dull task. That's all she'd done for the past week…work. Since their talk, she'd avoided him as much as she could, choosing instead to spend any time they might have had together with her head buried in a catalog. Oh, she was wonderful with Tyler. They'd gone Christmas shopping, gone to the Ramseys' to bake Christmas cookies, gone sledding. All of it when he was working, of course. Then, when he came home, she retreated to her catalogs. That had been their sole existence for seven long, stressful days. But he'd never once thought that she wouldn't come with them for a ride on the Christmas train.

Then, a little over an hour ago, she'd begged off, saying she had work to do. Tyler's response had been to turn sullen, then knock over and break a lamp. Sometimes it seemed like they were taking two steps forward, one step back. And this latest setback with the boy was definitely that one step back. In another week, after Christmas, the backward steps they were going to have to face would be insurmountable, he was afraid. But what choice did he have? Fallon didn't want him. Even after everything that had been said between them, she hadn't budged. But Tyler desperately needed him, which made his course clear.

It took an hour to board everyone, get them seated in close proximity to Santa, who was, after arguments and promises, Walt Graham, on his best behavior. New diet, being overseen and cooked by Catie, owner of Catie's Overlook. Promises to take his medications, being overseen by Neil, Eric and Gabby. Promises to exercise more, being overseen on daily walks with Pippa and Paige Ramsey. All part of the bargain to be Santa. "Ho, ho, ho!" he yelled as the train finally pulled away from the station and dozens of children sat on the edges of their seats, waiting to be called to visit Santa.

"I wish Fallon had come," Gabby said, handing her son, Bryce, to his dad while she made herself comfy on the seat by propping a pillow behind her back. "She's been working like crazy, and we're really not going to be doing much toward opening the hospital until after my baby arrives. She's been so stressed out lately, and I think this would have been good for her."

"Any excuse," James muttered, sounding as bitter as he felt. It was sinking in, all of it. And, yes, he did hurt. Badly. But he was also angry, and not about the decisions Fallon had made those months ago. He was angry for the ones she was making now...the ones that kept him from helping her get through this. That kept her from helping him get through this. They needed to be doing this together, dealing with it, healing, holding onto each other through the pain, but every day she seemed to pull away from him more and more. "If it hadn't been work, it would have been something else."

"Sounds like the two of you aren't doing very well right now."

"Actually, there's no such thing as the two of us. Ask Fallon. She'll be the first to tell you that we've gone our separate ways. It's what she's wanted all along and it finally happened. She got her way." She'd won, but they'd both lost.

Gabby exchanged wary glances with Dinah, who was sitting directly across from her. "I thought she'd been doing better lately," Dinah ventured. "I mean, the only times I've seen her these past several days she's been with Tyler. And she looks totally happy. They have a good time together, and I don't think she's faking that."

"She'll do anything in the world for Tyler." Just not for Tyler's dad, he thought.

"Well, give it time," Gabby consoled. "I'm sure things will work out. Fallon's come a long way in just these past weeks. After what she's been through, it's pretty amazing, when you come to think about it."

"Well, what I *don't* have is time. Being a single dad is taking up every spare minute I have. I'm either working or taking care of Tyler, which isn't a complaint. But it's a fact of life for me now, and while I'd rather be doing everything with Fallon, she's not budging." He didn't know if her friends knew, or even suspected, the reason, and it wasn't up to him to tell them.

"But you're still going after full custody of Tyler, aren't you?" Dinah asked.

"It's in the works. My investigator finally located Shelly, so the legal papers were served and now we're waiting to see if the court gets a response from her." He'd wanted to celebrate that next step with Fallon, but she'd turned him down. Told him to celebrate with his son.

"And?" Dinah pushed.

"Nothing, so far. The judge has given her another week to respond then we're moving forward with or without her." With or without Fallon, too. Truth was, he was happy about almost everything. Not having Fallon part of his happiness with Tyler dampened the mood, but didn't ruin it. He wasn't going to let that happen. However, this should have been the best time of his life, and in ways it was. Still, part of him was holding back. He knew that, and couldn't get past it because hoping for Fallon to change her mind was dragging him down. Nonetheless, this was about Tyler, now. Meaning he had to move on and hope Fallon followed someday. Or, learn to live without her if she didn't.

"Well, if there's anything Eric and I can do to help you, please don't hesitate to ask. Our daughters are infatuated with your son…" She pointed to the seat across the aisle where the three of them had their faces plastered to the glass, looking at all the magical Christmas decorations outside. Lights formed in images of ice skaters, and palaces, and dinosaurs.

Dinosaurs… Just like Matty Brower had promised. It was time to shake off the glum mood and enjoy the ride with his son. "I appreciate the offer, but so far Tyler and I are doing fine. He's still up and down with the behavioral issues, but even those seem to be evening out." Evening out like Fallon had said they would. Damn, he wished she'd come on this trip. If ever anybody needed a flashing red Christmas dinosaur to brighten her life, it was Fallon.

She couldn't wrap her mind around tongue depressors. Not today, not any more. The job was nice to have, it gave her a sense of purpose, but it was also filling her with such longing to return to nursing. This evening, she was particularly restless. She'd wanted to go on the Christmas train but, truly, she didn't belong there. It was for the children, and their parents or grandparents. She wasn't a parent. She didn't have a child, didn't want to sit on a train full of parents who had their children. It would have hurt so much. More than that, she would be losing Tyler, soon. And James. So much loss for her Christmas, she just couldn't put on the act tonight. Not even for Tyler's sake. This was the way it was meant to be but she'd never counted on it hurting so much. Never counted on feeling so empty.

Well, she'd made her choices. The ones in the past, the ones now. *Her choices.* That's what she'd have to keep telling herself. Because James…what he'd said. She did want to believe that, did want, with all her heart, to trust that. "But it's what you wanted," she reminded herself as she stared at the Christmas tree, trying to forget. Yet she couldn't. Because the harder she tried, the more she thought about James, about the things he'd said. There'd

been times these past days when she'd been on the verge
of convincing herself that he was totally wrong about everything, telling her she was afraid to let someone help
her, that she found it easier to be alone than have someone
there to help her. At those times she almost believed he
had been lashing out at her because he'd been hurt. Then
she'd think about James, remember the reasons she'd fallen
in love with him so quickly, so deeply, and realize that he
never lashed out unfairly at anyone. And that he had deep,
thoughtful perception. When she let herself remember
that, the thoughts that always followed were how he was
right. Right about everything. Then her gut would knot,
knowing how wrong she'd been.

But making it right? It scared her to death. She didn't
know how. Didn't want to feel the excruciating pain
again.

So tonight she was alone, staring at the tree. A beautiful
tree. Tyler had been adding ornaments daily, some he'd
bought, others he'd made. She loved these days with him,
wanted more. Hoped that James would allow her some
visitations, too. In fact, she was positioning a few of Tyler's
hand-made ornaments front and center when the phone
rang. It was Emoline Putters, in a panic.

"Don't know what to do," she cried. "We've got Dr.
McGinnis on call, and she can't leave the hospital…"

"Slow down," Fallon said. "Take a deep breath. Start
at the beginning."

Emoline's deep breath was audible over the phone. "It's
the train," she finally said. Then paused.

In that pause, a million bad scenarios passed through
Fallon's mind. She held her breath, trying not to leap
ahead, trying hard to hold to the moment. "What about
the train?" she asked the older woman.

"They turned the bend at Hubbard's Creek, started up

the incline there. You know how it gets steep for a while then levels off before it gets steep again. They got to the part that levels off, and…"

Fallon shut her eyes, pictured the terrain. Steep rock face to the right, a small shoulder to the left then a drop-off into the river. Most of the ride was on even ground, but this was one of two places where the lay of the land was a little dicey. Probably not so much for a modern locomotive, but for the antiquated Christmas train…

"Anyway, they started up the second incline…"

She pictured that incline. Not too steep, but steep enough to slow down the train.

"Avalanche off Daphne's Pointe. Hit part of the train. Buried it."

Emoline's voice trailed off. Or maybe it was Fallon's mind, already on course for something else. "Did it stay on the tracks?" she asked pointedly. "Did the train stay on the tracks?" Worst case scenario, it had been shoved off the tracks and toppled over the edge. Maybe all the way down into the river.

"Don't know," Emoline said. "It just happened a minute ago. I called you first."

"Any communication from anyone on the train?" Unlikely, due to all the mountains.

"Not so far."

"Is the train completely covered with snow, or is any of it visible?"

"Don't know anything yet. Except we need you here. Need you to be in charge. You're the only one, Fallon…"

She didn't even hesitate when she responded. Because, yes, James was right. People depended on her. "Put out all the normal calls. Get all the rescue crews we have mobilized, call everyone who's not on shift back to the hospital.

I'm on my way." For the next ten minutes, trying to keep her mind on the road as she maneuvered through all the icy turns and curves, she caught her thoughts drifting off to James, and Tyler. They were on that train! Trapped, maybe hurt. Maybe… "Dear God," she whispered, forcing her concentration back on the road. "Take care of them. Please, take care of them."

The lights were out, and the little pot-bellied stove at the rear of the train car had long since been extinguished for fear that fumes could back up into the train car, cause carbon monoxide poisoning without proper ventilation. There was no way of knowing if this was the only car trapped or if the entire train had been buried. Naturally, his cellphone didn't work, but James kept trying for a signal anyway. Punching in Fallon's number, over and over. Finding some comfort in knowing that even though she wasn't answering, she was out there, somewhere. Or maybe it was simply that the glow from his phone was reassuring. Presently it, along with the glows from other phones, was the only thing that kept them from sitting in pitch blackness.

"When can we get off?" Tyler whined.

"In a while," he answered. Same answer for the last hour. Same answer all the parents were giving their children.

"But I'm cold. And I want some hot chocolate."

Me too, James thought as he pulled Tyler closer to him fully prepared to have Tyler push him away. Which was what he always did when he was grumpy. But this time he wasn't pushing away. If anything, he seemed to be clinging harder and harder. "When we get off the train, you can have a gallon of hot chocolate. Two gallons, if you can hold that much."

"What's a gallon?" Tyler asked.

Paige and Pippa, sitting on the other side of the aisle with their parents, both giggled. "It's like what the milk comes in," their united voices rang out. "That's a gallon."

"Is it?" Tyler asked James.

"The ladies are right," James responded, once again flipping open his cellphone. Still no bars. Still no contact. But a little light was good and he dialed her number anyway.

Once again, nothing connected, so he settled back into his seat, staring into that light for a few moments. By now the rescue operation would have been called. Of course, all those in charge of mountain rescue were right here on the train with him. But that didn't bother him so much because by now Fallon would be in charge. And here he was, depending on that strength in her he'd come so close to criticizing.

"I need to get up and have a look at the scene," Fallon told Jess Weldon, one of the locals, who owned a helicopter. "Need to see what we're dealing with before we do anything." It was dark, no one had any idea as to the extent of the damage. But she couldn't put any kind of plan into action until she made the proper assessments and that, it seemed, was what everybody expected her to do.

"It's waiting for you," Jess said. "Any time you're ready."

"I know," she said, fighting against the panic welling up in her. She was perfectly content to never fly again. Walking, driving, taking a bus…all fine and dandy. But not lifting up off the ground. "Is there a road up there?"

"There is, but it will take you an hour, if you can even get through. It's probably not been cleared since the last hard snow, and I'm betting you'll probably come across a tree or two down on the road."

"So flying's the only way," she said, not to Jess but to convince herself.

"Unless you want to waste half the night, it is."

"Then all I have to do is…" Her hands started shaking. "Is get into the helicopter, fasten myself in, and…" And think of James and Tyler. And all her friends. They were counting on her now. Everybody in White Elk was counting on her, and here she was, working on a good case of nausea. She shut her eyes for a moment, trying to steady her unraveling nerves, but in the darkness behind her eyes she could see James and Tyler very clearly. "All I have to do is get in," she said resolutely. And that's exactly what she did. She marched to the helicopter, climbed into the seat, fastened herself in, and folded her hands in her lap as it lifted off into the darknight. Forcing herself to breathe. Forcing herself to concentrate on what had to be done.

Five minutes later, five minutes that felt like an eternity to Fallon, Jess was hovering over Daphne's Pointe, shining his spotlight down on the train. Or what should have been a train. The old locomotive and the first two cars were not visible at all, and only the tail end of the caboose could be seen. Those who'd been riding in the caboose were standing on the tracks, waving. Somehow the caboose had separated from the rest of the train and they'd managed to get out safely. That was a blessing.

The second blessing came when she saw that the rest of the train was on the tracks. Good news she radioed immediately to the hospital.

"Can I have a look at the side of the rock?" she asked after she was sure that the entire train was still upright. "Because what concerns me is that if we bring in crews to dig out the train, we might put them at risk from another avalanche."

"First avalanche we've had in these parts for fifty years," Jess said, bringing the helicopter round to a better spot. Once there, he turned his spotlight on the side of the mountain looming directly above the train. "Damned shame it had to happen just as the Christmas train was passing through."

While she wasn't an engineer, Fallon didn't rule out the possibility that the train was the reason the snow had broken loose and plummeted off the mountain. They'd had unseasonably warm weather, followed by several snowfalls, then warm weather, followed by snow again. The constant changing, plus the vibration of the train, seemed as good an explanation as any for what had happened. Only thing was, any more activity was likely to set off another avalanche, cover the train even more than it already was. And already Fallon was worried about the amount of oxygen inside the train cars. She had no reason to think that there would have been injuries as a result, but every fiber of her being screamed of suffocation because the train looked sealed shut inside a white mountain!

"I need an engineer who can figure out if the rest of the mountain's going to come down on us when we begin the rescue," she shouted to the group of people loitering in the hospital hall, waiting for instructions on what to do. "And I need someone who can tell me about the train car…what kind of timeline we're talking about on the oxygen situation."

Emoline stood off to the side, her hands jittery, her eyes full of tears as she took hasty notes.

"I want the best climbers we can find in White Elk, and notify the forestry service to respond, and I need…"

Strength. Dear God, she needed strength. There were so many people to rescue. If only James were here to help her through this. "Also call the avalanche center and tell them we need all the help that we can get, that we may have up to a hundred people trapped in those cars.

"How long's it been?" she asked Emoline.

"Just over an hour. Jackie Peterson called it in. He was watching the train from the opposite ridge. Saw it happen."

"Well, the good news is, we've got some people out on the tracks—they got out of the caboose. We need to get them out of there as fast as we can."

"I'll do that," said one of the volunteers, Mark Anderson.

She remembered him from the restaurant.

"I'll go with him," George Fitzhenry volunteered. "And take my crew." He was one of the senior members of the White Elk Mountain Rescue Team. "I'll also see about getting a bulldozer loaded up and transported down there. Maybe get another one coming in from the opposite side." He flipped open his phone and started dialing. "The back-up engine for the Christmas train should be available, so I'll have somebody go get it ready."

"They won't have much time," Mark Anderson whispered in her ear. "A few hours. But without fresh oxygen, and with all the carbon dioxide they're exhaling while they're sealed in…"

"It's going to take a miracle, isn't it?"

"I prefer to believe in skill," he said, quite rigidly. "Let the believers have their miracles. I'll rely on my skills."

"Then I hope you've got some mighty good skills because, at the end of the day, when they run out, we'll all be praying for a miracle. And that will include you too, Mark."

In the course of the next two minutes Fallon ordered out the rescue team's emergency lights, and put out a general call through White Elk that if anyone had any kind of generator-based lighting, or kerosene or propane lighting, they needed it. She wasn't sure yet how to get it to the scene, but she knew that this was a rescue that had to have as much light on it as they could muster. Daylight would have been good. Unfortunately, they didn't have it. But she depended on the people here to do what was necessary. She *depended* on them… "James," she whispered. "You were right about everything.

"I'll be working from the field," she told Emoline, as she did a mental check. "There are enough people here, in the hospital, to handle whatever comes in. And I'd feel better on the scene, directing operations from there." She'd feel closer to James and Tyler.

"You handle what you have to, any way you have to," Emoline said, batting away a tear. "We know you'll take care of this. You're the only one…"

An ominous distinction. One she didn't want, yet one she couldn't refuse. James was on that car. And Tyler. People she loved. People she didn't want to spend the rest of her life without. She'd already suffered so much loss, and the most excruciating pain…the one she feared most… was the loss of even more. She knew that now. And while every available avalanche expert and rescue team in the area converged on White Elk, she couldn't put aside the fact that she loved James and Tyler with all her heart and she'd made a huge mistake, turning away from them. *She did need them.* They would make her whole again. All these months, pushing people away, pushing James away… it had always been about her. Her fears, her denials, her pain. Not about James. Now she had to tell him. He had to know she'd been wrong, and he'd been right all along.

And all the time she'd wasted, trying to find ways to push him away… "We've got to get them, Emoline. That's all there is to it. We've got to get them." When they did, all she wanted was to collapse into James's arms and lean on him for a while…for ever.

At the two-hour point, Fallon went back out to the field. She needed to see the scene again. Needed to see if anything had changed, needed to direct all the people now coming in to help. So she turned over hospital preparation to half the handful of doctors who'd come in, and took the other half of them with her. Along with more than a hundred other volunteers. She wasn't sure what she would do with all that many people but if the train was declared stable enough, she'd have every one of them digging by hand, if that's what it took.

"Don't give up, James," she whispered, running through the parking lot on her way back to the helicopter. "I can do this. I know I can do this." If ever there was a time she needed to believe in herself, to trust herself, this was it.

At the three-hour point, Fallon received the news she'd been waiting for. "We think it's an isolated incident, Miss O'Gara," Ben Lawson from the avalanche center told her. "My engineers are up top and don't see anything that looks like it's going to come down. The snow load that broke loose is fairly light, so we should be able to move it off pretty quickly once we get the equipment out here. I do need to advise you that it will be a safer job for the rescuers if we wait until daylight. I commend all the people here for the way they're trying to light up the area, but it's not good enough, and I can't recommend a night-time rescue. It's too risky."

She glanced across the canyon at all the lights lit up on the opposite ridge. It looked festive, like White Elk had joined together, bringing every light they could find, just to have a party. Not to rescue the Christmas train and all its passengers. "They're going to run out of oxygen," she said gravely.

"They should make it until morning."

"Should?"

"It's hard to calculate."

"Well, *should* isn't good enough."

"Maybe not for you, but it's still not advisable to start some kind of haphazard rescue. It puts the rescuers at as big a risk as the people trapped in the train. And in all probability, like I said, the oxygen should hold out until we can get to them."

"And like I said, *in all probability* isn't good enough, Mr. Lawson." The tough decision was about to weigh down on her. She could already feel it pressing on her shoulders, feel all the people depending on her now crowding in. "I have to have a guarantee. A one hundred percent promise that if we don't go in tonight, every single person on board will come out fine and dandy in the morning when we finally do get to them. Can you give me that?"

He shook his head. "You need to know all the variables. That's all I'm telling you."

"And I appreciate that, but the only variable you need to know is that those people trapped in the train have to be rescued *now*. Not tomorrow. And it's my decision to make." She understood the risks both ways, but she also understood all those variables he talked about. And the one variable he didn't know was the volunteers…she knew them, trained them, worked with them, trusted them. Depended on them. More than that, they trusted her. It was a variable Ben Lawson couldn't even fathom. "My decision is that we're going to do it *now*."

* * *

"So, what's the status?" she asked George Fitzhenry.

"We got fifteen people off the tracks, and they're on their way back to the station. Walking. Cold. Shaken up. But glad to be alive. And, no injuries."

"That's good. What about the bulldozer?"

"We're in some luck there. We're about thirty minutes out, having one brought in from White Elk, and Aspen Grove is sending one up from their end of the tracks. It's got an ETA of about an hour. They're also sending in volunteers with it."

She glanced up at the helicopter overhead. Jess was back up again, hovering, keeping watch. His engine was loud. Could James hear it? Would he know that was her trying to rescue him? "Radio Jess for me. Tell him to set down in the meadow, that I need to go up top again and have another look for myself."

"At what?"

"The safety of going over the edge. We need people on top of the train. It's all well and good to dig from both ends, but we've got to get the top cleared so we can get some windows open. Ben Lawson said it looks stable to his people, but it has to look stable to me before I send anybody over the edge. And, George, I want you up there with me. By rights, you're the lead on this operation and I need your expertise on this."

"Maybe by rights, but I think I'd be barking orders at a crowd that's waiting for your orders, Fallon. They listen to me, but they depend on you, and that's the difference. But I'll go up with you. Give me five minutes to secure my team down here. OK?"

Five minutes where she wanted to dig at the snow with her fingers.

"When are they going to turn on the lights?"

James looked at the cellphone display. Four hours now,

and nothing. He'd expected…no, he'd hoped for..something. A tap from outside, an errant cellphone message getting through. Anything. But they'd been sitting in the dark for four long hours, getting colder as well as running out of oxygen. Neil had managed to find a rescue tank in a supply closet and had it on hand for Gabby, who was too close to her due date to suffer any kind of oxygen deprivation. Other than that, all they could do was sit and wait, and not panic. Panic sped up oxygen consumption. Theoretically, they could exist here for days, if they had oxygen to breathe. They were safe, no injuries, no one suffering any real ills. And there was plenty of cold hot chocolate and cookies to dole out in moderation over the course of several days.

"I know she's working on it," Eric said from across the aisle, where he was huddled with his wife and daughters.

"She's got good instincts," Neil added. "She'll get this figured out."

But in time? James wanted to believe that Fallon could pull out a miracle, but even Fallon had her limitations. "You knew I wanted to marry her, didn't you?" he said into the dark, knowing all his friends were listening. Somehow, talking about Fallon brought her closer. Made him, and probably everybody else, feel more confident. Most especially made him believe with all his heart that Fallon would pull out the miracle. That she *was* the miracle. "That's why I originally applied for the job here, to be closer to her. She's stubborn, you know. I knew it was going to take some work." It still *would* take some work. And once they got off this train…

In the dark, as the silent agreement spread over them, everyone chuckled at their own recollections of Fallon's stubbornness.

"Haven't given up, though," James continued. "I thought I was going to, that it was time for me to move on with my life. Fallon has this idea that she's better off alone, but she's wrong about that. So once she gets us out of this, I'm going to start all over and this time do what it takes to convince her that she's wrong about that and I'm right." And he *was* right. Fallon needed him, and Tyler. She knew it, and she denied it, and she fought it because she was afraid they'd leave her, like her mother had. Like her baby had. What she'd done during those months when she'd been clinging to a futile pregnancy... He couldn't fault her for that because he would have been fighting to save *her* while she'd braved the fight to keep her baby. That's the Fallon he loved. But *that* Fallon wouldn't have given in to him, wouldn't have ever thought that *she* came first, not as long as her baby was still alive inside her. Not as long as she was holding onto hope. That, too, was the Fallon he loved. She'd done the only thing she could do, and hated herself for it. But now it was time to find a way to help her, to make her feel safe again, to convince her that the people who loved her wouldn't leave her. That he wouldn't leave her. When she understood that, her true healing would begin. And as hard as she would fight to push him away, he was prepared to fight even harder to stay.

"What are you right about?" Tyler asked.

"That the three of us should be a family." He'd sworn not to tell Tyler until the custody arrangement was in place, but he couldn't wait any longer. Fallon had waited too long to tell him what he should have known and they were both reeling from the devastation that had caused. He wasn't going to wait any longer to tell Tyler because Tyler did have the right to know he was wanted, that he was being fought for. The way Fallon would know as soon as he could tell her. "I'm working very hard right now to have you come live with me for ever. All the time, in that new house I'm buying for us."

"The great big one on the hill?" he asked.

"The great big house on the hill. Would you like to live there?"

Tyler didn't answer, but James felt his usual shrug. And smiled. That was as good as a yes.

From across the aisle, Dinah strangled back a sob. "That's so...nice," she said.

"We'll help you," Gabby said from behind him. "Whatever it takes, let us know."

It would take a change of heart from Fallon. And that was solely up to him to achieve. But it was nice knowing his friends were on his side.

Ben Lawson was right about the condition of the snow above the train, and it was such a relief. "It looks like most of the snow rolled off," Fallon said, aiming her light down the cliff. "And I think we can get down on top of that train."

"I've got eight strong climbers, all of them ready to go," George Fitzhenry said, clicking on his walkie-talkie. "Give us an hour, and we'll be down there."

"I want to go, too," Fallon told him.

"That's a long way down, Fallon. I know you're a strong climber, but are you up to it? I mean, it couldn't have been easy going up in the helicopter the way you did. I'm concerned that once you get to the edge of the cliff..."

"I can do this, George," she said. "Everything important in my life is in that train, and I have to go down there. And I'm going to be first, because I don't want a lot of weight on top of the cars until I've evaluated them. So, what, maybe send two people per car at first?"

"We can do that," George said. "But we're going to have to get some lights up here before anybody goes over the edge."

"That's the easy part," Fallon said, waving for Jess Weldon. "Jess," she said. "One hour. Get as many working lights up on Daphne's Pointe as you can.

"That other doc at the hospital…his name's Anderson. Mark Anderson…"

"What about him?"

"He just radioed me. Said he's a licensed helicopter pilot. Wants to know if we can use him."

"Eric has a helicopter…"

"It'll speed things up, having us both bringing up lights."

And speed was what she needed. "Tell him to do it. Also, I don't want any of the lights on the opposite ridge moved. We need them there as much as we need them up here."

"White Elk's bulldozer is five minutes out," George informed her.

"Then I guess I need to figure out what they'll do." She trotted after Jess Weldon, leaving George on the peak as she went back to the plateau below that was the marshaling area for everything taking place. After a fast consult with the engineers, it was agreed that the first task would be to get the caboose off the track. Dig it out, pull it away. While that was being done, engineers and experienced mountain rescuers were evaluating the stability of the train itself on the tracks. Best scenario was that is was fully upright, not tilting or skew in any way.

With things squared away there, Fallon was back to the helicopter. It was hard to believe that only a few hours ago an entire army couldn't have dragged her into one, and now there was no fear. It was what she had to do.

No thoughts to do otherwise. And this time, when Jess dropped her off up top, her next task was to get the climbers ready to go down. She being one of the climbers. No fear, again because when she allowed herself a moment to fix on the faces of James and Tyler there wasn't a question in her mind. Or her heart.

"What kind of casualties are you expecting?" one of the climbers asked her.

She wasn't thinking in terms of casualties. Sure, she'd alerted several hospitals in Salt Lake City to be on standby. And she'd arranged for a dozen ambulances to come in from all the surrounding villages and towns. But she wasn't expecting casualties. Didn't have room for that scenario in her mind.

"None," she said. Either everyone would survive with little to no injury. Or everyone would… But she couldn't say that out loud. If she lost James and Tyler…that was a tragedy from which she'd never recover. It put everything into place in her life. In that instant she'd heard about the train, she'd known…everything. "I'm not expecting any casualties," she said, praying it was true.

Tyler stirred against James's side. "I hear Santa," Tyler said.

It was the first thing anybody had said for nearly half an hour. People were uncomfortable and cold. Children were restless, adults were finally giving in to fear. People in the train car had talked at first and the mood had become quite jovial. Eventually, the talk died down to whispers, reverted to couples and families saying the things that needed to be said in their last hours. People were trying to make their peace.

Which was what he had to do with Tyler, James decided, now that Tyler was awake again. No more secrets.

Not ever. "When your mother brought you to me, I didn't know you were my son, Tyler. She'd never told me."

"Donnie used to be my dad."

"But not your real dad. He was your dad because he was married to your mom. But I was always your *real* dad, from the minute you were born. And I would have been there, Tyler. If I'd known you were my son, I would have always been there."

"Why didn't you know?"

Such a hard question. One he had to get right, so he thought for a moment. "I think your mother just forgot to tell me," he finally said. Someday, when Tyler was older, he'd understand. For now, this was enough. "Like the way you sometimes forget things."

"Oh," he said, totally accepting, then snuggled a little closer. "Well, I don't think Santa forgot, because I think he's coming to get us now."

The optimism of a child. It made him proud, and broke his heart for the things he'd missed, and the things he might never have now. He cleared his throat, swallowed back the emotion boiling up inside him. Now it was time to ask because he had to know, had to hear it from Tyler. "Do you want me for your dad?" he asked, a huge lump in his throat almost choking the words. "Do you want to stay here and live with me all the time now?"

"Sure."

It was a matter-of-fact *sure*, not an excited one, not an emotional one. But for James it was the single best word he'd ever heard in his lifetime, because Tyler had just accepted him. Now, if only Fallon would.

"And can I have Fallon for my new mom?" Tyler asked.

Across the aisle and behind him, the strangled sobs

from Gabby and Dinah rang out in the dark. "I'm working on it, Tyler. I'm really working on it."

"Good, and maybe I can help you, Dad." The word *dad* came so easily from him. Like maybe he'd practiced it, or been prepared for it? "Can you hear Santa *now*?" Tyler continued.

As James swiped at the tears streaming down his face, glad he was sitting in total darkness, he almost believed he, too, heard Santa. Then suddenly the train rocked… People inside gasped, several of the women sobbed. Fear of the unknown, that's what it was. They were frightened by the unknown. But he knew what the unknown was and, for sure, it wasn't Santa. It was the woman he loved.

Nothing could have stopped her from going over the edge when the time came. No person on earth, not even her own fear. In fact, she didn't even think about the height, or how she would be practically dangling in mid-air from the top of a mountain cliff when the OK was given to proceed. She simply lowered herself down, keeping her mind focused on the task ahead. The old Fallon was back, and Fallon was glad to embrace her. The fit was perfect, it felt good. Felt great.

Fallon was holding onto the ropes for dear life. It had been so many hours now, she'd lost track. But they were so close she could almost feel James's presence. "How should we proceed?" she asked George Fitzhenry.

"I think what we need to do is clear a section all the way across the train top and move it down the side. Get a window exposed, break it open. Each of the cars, and the engine. Once we do that, the rest won't matter. It'll probably take a while to get everybody out. And if we do have any serious injuries inside, or if Gabby chooses now to have that baby, we can deal with the rescue."

Progress in getting the area cleared took longer than Fallon expected because they had to take care not to cause too much rocking to the train. Digging out the snow, little by little, took an interminably long time. But finally a window was exposed.

"I can't see anything," she told George. She was trying to see inside. Suspended in the air, swaying with the mountain winds that were picking up as the night grew later and longer. But all she could see was blackness.

"Take the hatchet, and knock it out," George called to her. "Knock on the window a few times so people will move away, then break it."

Which was exactly what she did. One hatchet, one hard whack, and the window shattered into shards. Fallon didn't even wait for all the pieces to land before she screamed, "James! Tyler! I love you! Can you hear me? I love you! Nothing else matters. I want to marry you. *Both of you.* I want to marry you!"

"See," Tyler told his dad. "I told you I heard Santa."

"The best Santa I've ever heard," James whispered.

All around him, the people in the train car broke into spontaneous applause, not for the rescue but for James and Fallon.

It took nearly twelve more hours to get everyone safely home and pull the train off the tracks. The total casualty count—zero. People were cold, hungry, achy, but that was all. Days later, on Christmas Eve, most of White Elk gathered in the town square to sing carols and celebrate a miracle.

As for Fallon, she'd spent the past few days huddled under a blanket on the couch in front of the fireplace, barely taking her eyes off the people she loved most in the world. Clinging to them, and happy to do so.

People stopped by the house at all hours of the day and night. They brought food and gifts, or simply came for a short visit, and they were invited in. Welcomed. And when she thought about how things could have turned out so badly, and how many of her dearest friends would have been affected…well, she'd never take her friendships for granted again. She was a lucky woman because the people of White Elk were true friends. One of the best gifts of her Christmas was coming to understand the meaning of true friendship. The best gift of all, though, had arrived in the form of a letter from the court stating that Tyler's mother was relinquishing all custody, unconditionally. Maybe that was the only way Shelly knew how to show that she loved her son. Or maybe it was simply about convenience.

"We could always adopt," she whispered to James, as they were making plans for their future. Part of those plans being Emoline Putters's house. A place to start over, a place to heal *together*. And that would take time, and more pain. They understood that. But together it was something they could face. Together it was something they would work through and find a deeper meaning in their love. Fallon accepted that with all her heart. Because she trusted James. Because she depended on James.

"Or be grateful for the family we have," James said. "Because the three of us are pretty awesome together." They were watching Tyler contemplate all the gifts under the Christmas tree. "I don't need to have a dozen children to make me happy, Fallon. I know that's what you thought, maybe even what I thought. But sitting in that train all those hours, I had a lot of time to think. And what I came to realize was that with Tyler, and you, I have everything in the world I need to make me happy. Everything I want. And telling you that I wanted a dozen children was… arrogant."

"You're not arrogant," she said.

"Well, maybe not arrogant so much as unrealistic. But there's something about being stuck on a freezing train and slowly running out of oxygen that really grounds you. Really makes you take a hard look at your life. I wanted you before, Fallon. Have never stopped loving you, and won't stop loving you, no matter what kind of fears you have about that. We'll work through the past. There's still a lot of emotion there, a lot of pain, but we have time to make it better."

"I know," she said.

"Do you really?"

"I had a lot of time to think in those hours, too. And the one thing that kept coming back to me was you. I know you, James. Know your heart. You were right. It *was* me I was running away from, not you. Everything hurt so bad that I just didn't know what to do. I was so...confused. Lost."

"But I've found you, Fallon."

"And I want to stay found."

He tightened his hold on her, and she sighed contentedly. "I'm still stubborn. That's not going to change."

"I'm counting on it."

"And Tyler? Have you talked to him about...us?"

"Actually, he's the one who talked to me. Asked if you were going to be his new mom. In his matter-of-fact way, of course."

"With a shrug?" she asked.

"Only the way Tyler can shrug. One little gesture and my whole life fell into place."

"Poor James." Fallon laughed. "Treated with indifference the way most children treat their parents."

"A cruel dose of reality. And the best one I can think of."

"But look how happy he is now. That's all that counts,

you know. We have him, we'll take care of him, and we'll get him through whatever problems he'll have because of his past. The three of us…three's so much better than one." Nothing about Tyler's past was going to change. But that part of his life was over. Like so much of her past life had finally been put behind her. She was wanted now. Someone…two someones…finally, truly wanted Fallon O'Gara. And Fallon O'Gara finally, truly, knew that. "Want to build a snowman?" she asked her men.

James moaned, Tyler groaned.

"OK," she conceded, "let's play a game. I know it's not Christmas yet, but I'm pretty sure there's a game system under the tree. Santa dropped it off early so he wouldn't have to carry it around when he goes out later tonight, so…"

Tyler ran out from behind the tree, where he'd been organizing the packages. "Which one?" he squealed.

"The red one. But be careful you don't…" Words of caution on deaf ears. Tyler dove after the package, effectively knocking the tree flat on the floor, with him underneath.

"You OK?" James called, jumping up to rescue him.

"I found it. And it's just what Santa promised me."

Laughing, Fallon joined James, and both of them simply stared down at the mess. "We could just leave it," she said, snaking her hand around his waist. "Maybe if Santa stops by again he'll clean it up for us."

James bent to whisper in her ear. "I think Santa has something entirely different in mind for his next visit tonight. If we can ever get Tyler to go to bed. And somebody invites Santa upstairs."

"Santa's invited." They'd slept together, *all three of them*, for the past days. Mostly because she didn't want either of her men out of her sight, not even for a little while. But now it was time to move on. She knew that, understood it in profound ways. "Then I think we need to get that game set up and wear him out." She glanced anxiously at the stairs. It had been too long. It was time to rectify that. "Fast!"

"Are you sure, Fallon? I'm a patient man. I can wait."

"But I'm not a patient woman, and I can't. No more wasting precious time, James. Not ever again."

"Well, in that case…"

She expected a kiss, but what she got was a tug into the heart of the Christmas tree mess, first to retrieve their son, second to get his game. Time was being wasted and she did, indeed, have something to celebrate tonight. "I'm going in," James said, dropping to his hands and knees, blowing her a kiss then smiling. "Wish me luck."

Laughing, she tossed him an air kiss. "In case you don't come out, I love you. I always have. Always will."

"I know," James said, crawling partially underneath the tree then latching onto Tyler's hand. "I always knew you loved me. No matter what happened, I knew that, Fallon. And I've always loved you. I didn't always go about it the right way, but my feelings have never changed."

From James's lips to her heart. It was the best Christmas gift—ever!

You need to see the whole view, Fallon. That's where you'll find your happiness. Such wise words from Edith Weston. She did see the whole view now. It was a beautiful view. Perfect. And it was truly where she *had* found her happiness.

MILLS & BOON®
HAVE JOINED FORCES WITH THE LEANDER TRUST AND LEANDER CLUB TO HELP TO DEVELOP TOMORROW'S CHAMPIONS

We have produced a stunning calendar for 2011 featuring a host of Olympic and World Champions (as they've never been seen before!). Leander Club is recognised the world over for its extraordinary rowing achievements and is committed to developing its squad of athletes to help underpin future British success at World and Olympic level.

'All my rowing development has come through the support and back-up from Leander. The Club has taken me from a club rower to an Olympic Silver Medallist. Leander has been the driving force behind my progress'

RIC EGINGTON – Captain, Leander Club Olympic Silver, Beijing, 2009 World Champion.

Please send me ☐ **calendar(s) @ £8.99 each plus £3.00 P&P** (FREE postage and packing on orders of 3 or more calendars despatching to the same address).

I enclose a cheque for £ _____ made payable to Harlequin Mills & Boon Limited.

Name _____

Address _____

_____ Post code _____

Email _____

Send this whole page and cheque to:
Leander Calendar Offer
Harlequin Mills & Boon Limited
Eton House, 18-24 Paradise Road, Richmond TW9 1SR

All proceeds from the sale of the 2011 Leander Fundraising Calendar will go towards the Leander Trust (Registered Charity No: 284631) – and help in supporting aspiring athletes to train to their full potential.

Medical Romance™

THE MIDWIFE'S CHRISTMAS MIRACLE
by Jennifer Taylor

Midwife Lucy Harris has no trouble believing Dr Max Curtis's playboy reputation! She longs to be immune to his dark good looks, but Max's tenderness towards his tiny patients thaws her frozen heart… As the village's festive lights twinkle, Lucy finds her thoughts turn from medicine…to marriage!

THE DOCTOR'S SOCIETY SWEETHEART
by Lucy Clark

Socialite Emmy is determined to show her boss Dr Dartagnan Freeman that she's more dedicated to triage than tiaras! Before long Dart discovers that Emmy is a warm, compassionate doctor… Could Australia's sweetheart be bringing his heart back to life?

**On sale from 3rd December 2010
Don't miss out!**

Available at WHSmith, Tesco, ASDA, Eason and all good bookshops
www.millsandboon.co.uk

All the magic you'll need this Christmas...

When **Daniel** is left with his brother's kids, only one person can help. But it'll take more than mistletoe before **Stella** helps him...

Patrick hadn't advertised for a housekeeper. But when **Hayley** appears, she's the gift he didn't even realise he needed.

Alfie and his little sister know a lot about the magic of Christmas – and they're about to teach the grown-ups a much-needed lesson!

Available 1st October 2010

www.millsandboon.co.uk

★ ★ ★

MILLS & BOON®

are proud to present our...

Book of the Month ★

★ The Accidental Princess
by Michelle Willingham
from Mills & Boon® Historical

Etiquette demands Lady Hannah Chesterfield ignore
the shivers of desire Lieutenant Michael Thorpe's
wicked gaze provokes, but her unawakened body
clamours for his touch… So she joins Michael on
an adventure to uncover the secret of his birth—
is this common soldier really a prince?

Available 5th November

Something to say about our
Book of the Month?
Tell us what you think!

millsandboon.co.uk/community
facebook.com/romancehq
twitter.com/millsandboonuk

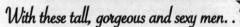

2 FREE BOOKS
AND A SURPRISE GIFT

We would like to take this opportunity to thank you for reading this Mills & Boon® book by offering you the chance to take TWO more specially selected books from the Medical™ series absolutely FREE! We're also making this offer to introduce you to the benefits of the Mills & Boon® Book Club™—

- **FREE home delivery**
- **FREE gifts and competitions**
- **FREE monthly Newsletter**
- **Exclusive Mills & Boon Book Club offers**
- **Books available before they're in the shops**

Accepting these FREE books and gift places you under no obligation to buy, you may cancel at any time, even after receiving your free books. Simply complete your details below and return the entire page to the address below. You don't even need a stamp!

YES Please send me 2 free Medical books and a surprise gift. I understand that unless you hear from me, I will receive 5 superb new stories every month including two 2-in-1 books priced at £5.30 each and a single book priced at £3.30, postage and packing free. I am under no obligation to purchase any books and may cancel my subscription at any time. The free books and gift will be mine to keep in any case.

Ms/Mrs/Miss/Mr _____ Initials _____

Surname _____

Address _____

_____

_____ Postcode _____

E-mail _____

Send this whole page to: Mills & Boon Book Club, Free Book Offer, FREEPOST NAT 10298, Richmond, TW9 1BR